DISASTER AT DARK RIVER

Book Four

JERRY D. THOMAS

Pacific Press® Publishing Association
Nampa, Idaho
Oshawa, Ontario, Canada

112294

Editor: Aileen Andres Sox
Designer: Robert N. Mason
Illustration/Art Direction: Justinen Creative Group
Typeset in Century Old Style 13/17

Library of Congress Cataloging-in-Publication Data

Thomas, Jerry D., 1959-
    Disaster at Dark River and other stories/Jerry D. Thomas.
       p. cm. —(Great Stories for Kids; bk. 4)
    Summary: A collection of stories to help the reader deal with problems and make good decisions, in such areas as bullying, self-esteem, safety, keeping promises, living with your conscience, and more.
    ISBN 0-8163-1714-3 (pbk.)
    1. Conduct of life—Juvenile. 2. Christian life—Juvenile. 3. Children's stores, American. [1. Conduct of life. 2. Christian life. 3. Short stories.]
    I. Title. II. Series: Thomas, Jerry D., 1959-Great Stores for Kids: 4.
PZ7.T366954Di 1999
—dc21
                                      98-49752
                                           CIP
                                            AC

ISBN 0-8163-1714-3

99 00 01 02 03 • 5 4 3 2 1

Dedication

To all the little people who inspired these stories:

First, to my own wonderful children—Jonathan, Jennifer, and Jeremy—who aren't so little anymore. Not all the stories are about them—just the good ones.

And then to my brothers and sisters—in memory of the days when we were kids and of the escapades we shared. Also, to my nieces and nephews on both sides of the family—thanks for the stories you inspired.

Finally, to all the kids who will read these stories or hear them read. May the stories bring you smiles, laughter, help in difficult situations, hope for a bright tomorrow, and a belief in the never-ending love of God.

A few words of thanks:

To the management of Pacific Press for having the vision to publish this set.

To Aileen Andres Sox, who encouraged me from the beginning.

To Robert Mason for a design that will drag kids right into the pages.

To Lars and Kim Justinen and their creative group for the outstanding art that brings the stories to life.

And most of all, to my wife, Kitty, for her love and patient endurance while these stories were being written.

Contents

Just Plain Mean

Kick. Smack. Crash!

Before his mother's voice even reached his ears, Ollie was on the floor picking up the broken mug pieces. "Oliver Johnson, take that soccer ball outside, and don't bring it back in until you are through kicking it."

"Yes, ma'am. Sorry." For a few minutes, Ollie kicked the soccer ball against the front steps. He was smaller than most of the kids in his class at school, but his soccer kick was getting stronger all the time.

"Hey, try dribbling around it."

Ollie turned and smiled at his friend, Derek. "I could dribble around you," he said.

"Maybe," Derek admitted, "but you can't kick a goal against me." Derek's favorite position in soccer was goalie. He liked stopping other players' kicks. "Let's go down to the school and practice."

"I'll tell my mom." Ollie turned and yelled into an open

> Setting boundaries;
> dealing with hatred; self-esteem

window, "Mom, I'm going to the school with Derek to play soccer."

"Oliver, wait a minute," his mother called. From the doorway, she asked, "Don't you two have a math test tomorrow?"

"Mom, we'll have time to study later."

"I could come back and study with Ollie after we play, Mrs. Johnson," Derek offered.

"OK," she agreed, "but don't play long. And be careful."

The boys were down the street in a flash, kicking the ball back and forth. Their school was only a few blocks away.

"I'll make this goal for sure," Ollie shouted as he raced toward the soccer goal at the end of the field.

"No fair," Derek cried. "You got a head start."

Ollie kicked the ball into the net and raced away, raising his hands as if he had just won the game. Derek tossed it

back out. "Let's see you try that again."

After a few minutes, Ollie said, "I'm going to try a few with my left foot. My dad says that good soccer players can use either foot to kick goals."

As Ollie kicked, Derek asked, "Do you understand those word problems in math?"

Ollie dribbled as he talked. "They're pretty dumb. 'If Train A leaves South City at 1:00 going west, and Train B leaves North City at 2:00 going east, what time will it be when they crash?' "

"Time to get new trains!" Derek shouted. Ollie laughed and kicked a shot straight in. Derek was laughing so hard he missed it.

"Why don't they make up good word problems?" Derek said as he crawled into the net after the ball. "Like 'If a soccer ball is kicked at one hundred miles per hour directly at a math teacher, how long would it take to get a math test canceled?' "

"Hey, who's playing soccer down at that other field?" Ollie asked, pointing across the schoolyard.

Derek shaded his eyes and stared. "Uh-oh. It's Herk the Jerk and his friends."

"Who?"

"You know. That big kid from the other fifth-grade class."

Ollie remembered. "Is his name really Herk?"

Derek whispered as if what he had to say was a secret. "His real name is Herkimer. Don't ask me why his parents would do that to him. Anyway, he calls himself 'Hercules.' Most everyone else calls him 'Herk the Jerk.'

"Why?"

Derek laughed. "If you knew him, you'd know why. He loves to pick on other kids. He's just plain mean."

It wasn't long before Ollie found out for himself. When Derek kicked one over his head, Ollie chased it to the edge of the other field. The ball stopped right in front of Herk and his friends.

"Hey, could you kick it back?" he yelled as he ran toward them. No one moved. When he was just a few feet away, Herk stepped out and put his foot on the ball. Ollie stopped.

"This your ball?" Herk asked.

"Yes," Ollie said.

"Then go get it." With that, Herk kicked it as hard as he could away from the field. It bounced almost all the way to the school building.

"Hey, that's not . . ." Ollie started to say. Then the look on Herk's face made him close his mouth. He ran after his soccer ball. By the time he walked back, Derek was sitting at the side of the field. Herk and his friends were kicking shots at the goal.

"What happened? Why are you sitting here?"

Derek pointed to the field. "I was waiting for you, and they just took over. I saw what Herk did to your ball. He is a jerk."

Ollie stared out at the boys on the field. They were all bigger than he or Derek were.

"Let's go tell them we were here first," Derek said. But he seemed surprised when Ollie walked out onto the field. "Wait! Where are you going?"

Ollie said, "Let's just play down on the other end."

They had only kicked the ball back and forth a few times when Herk's ball flew between them, followed by Herk. "Hey, get off the field," he shouted as he stopped his ball.

"We were here first," Ollie said quietly.

Herk stomped over and stuck his face down next to Ollie's. "I said, get off the field, shrimp. Or I will kick you as far as I

kicked your stupid ball."

Ollie's mouth hung open, and he blinked his eyes a few times. Then he grabbed his ball and didn't stop running until he got home.

That evening at supper, his mom asked about school. "How is everything going?"

"OK, I guess. I'm ready for the math test," Ollie answered. Inside, he thought, *I'm sure glad Herk is in the other fifth-grade room.*

Two days later, Ollie's teacher made an announcement. "Class," Mrs. Appleby said, "we have a new class member. He transferred over from the other fifth-grade room."

Derek looked at Ollie with wide eyes.

"His name is . . . Herkimer Adams."

"Herk," Herk said from the back. "My name is Herk."

For a while, Ollie worried. But he forgot about Herk when

Mrs. Appleby began to hand out the math tests. He was proud to see the "A" on his paper.

"Many of you did very well on the test," Mrs. Appleby said. "Those who did may go out to recess early. The rest will stay here with me and review math."

Ollie and Derek lined up at the back of the room with the others. Then Ollie happened to glance toward Herk, who still sat in his seat.

With the look he got back, he knew that his troubles with Herk were just beginning.

Ollie in a Cage

Smack! The soccer ball flew toward the goal. Ollie raced after it, angling for another kick. He was the captain of one of the recess teams. The other captain had picked Herk. Everyone knew Herk could kick harder than anyone else in fifth grade.

Just as Ollie slowed to kick, something smashed into him from the side. He hit the ground as if he had been thrown from a truck.

"Oops," Herk said as he smiled wickedly, "I guess I ran into you, Polly." He turned and walked away.

"My name is Ollie," Ollie said as he staggered to his feet. "Mark," he called back to one of his teammates, "trade places with me."

The trade left Ollie playing in front of

Setting boundaries;
dealing with hatred; self-esteem

Ollie in a Cage

Derek, the goalie. "What happened?" Derek asked.

"Herk happened," Ollie answered. "He knocked me over."

"He sure doesn't like you," Derek said.

The ball rolled toward Ollie, and Herk was right behind it. Ollie ran up to block Herk's path to the goal. Herk didn't try to go around Ollie. Instead, he slowed down and kicked it as hard as he could. Right at Ollie.

Oooof. The ball smacked Ollie right in the stomach. He fell down and gasped, trying to breathe.

"Hey! You did that on purpose," Derek shouted as he ran out of the goal box. Everyone stopped playing to see what had happened.

"I was trying to kick a goal. If Polly can't take it, he shouldn't be playing." Herk trotted over to the soccer ball and kicked it into the empty net. "Our goal. We win," he said as he walked away.

Derek helped Ollie to his feet. "Are you OK?"

Ollie nodded. He was trying not to cry, but it really did hurt. Derek helped him to class as recess ended.

The next day, Herk was racing straight at Ollie again, dribbling the ball. Ollie held his ground, waiting for a chance to steal. Just as he got near, Herk shouted "Haa!" and acted as if he was kicking.

Without thinking, Ollie ducked and covered his stomach. Herk turned and blew right past him, scoring an easy goal. "What a wimp," Herk called. A lot of other kids laughed. Even Derek shook his head.

Ollie just walked away. It was the last time he played soccer that week.

"Ollie, you don't seem very happy tonight," Mom said that evening. "In fact, you haven't been yourself all week. You

haven't played soccer with Derek even once."

Ollie thought about explaining what was happening with Herk, but he was afraid his mother would think he was a wimp too. "I guess I've just been tired."

"Well, get to bed early then," she said. "Tomorrow, your dad will be home for the weekend. And we're going to the zoo with a picnic lunch."

The next morning, Ollie watched the monkeys swing through their cage. His mom and dad laughed as a big monkey chased a smaller one around the cage.

"Look at him go," Mr. Johnson said, as the little monkey swung across the top of the cage. Usually, Ollie liked to watch the monkeys as much as anyone. But today, it made him angry to see the little monkey being chased.

"Stop it!" he shouted at his parents. "Stop laughing. How do you think that little monkey feels?" His dad raised one eyebrow. Then he walked away. Ollie just stared at the monkey cage, not really seeing the monkeys at all. *I'm in trouble now*, he thought.

"Over here, guys," he heard his dad call. At a shaded picnic table, his dad held out a cold drink with a straw.

"OK, Oliver," he said, "your mother says that something has been bothering you all week. Something is certainly bothering you today. What's going on?"

Ollie closed his eyes. "There's a new kid in my class at school. His name is Herk." He told them about the math test and the soccer games. When he described being hit in the stomach, his mother gasped.

"Where was the teacher?" she started to ask, but Dad patted her arm, and she was quiet.

"And he calls me 'Polly.' So now I don't play soccer at school or after school." He blinked hard to keep the tears back.

"Oliver, are you afraid of Herk?" Dad asked.

Ollie just said, "He's a lot bigger than I am."

"It's all right to admit that you are afraid. It's normal to be afraid of someone who can hurt you." Dad paused for a sip from his own drink. "But there's something we need to learn here. Oliver, why do they have bars around the monkey cages?"

Ollie just stared at him.

"Why do they have cages or pens for all these animals?"

"To keep them in?"

Dad laughed. "Well, yes. But the cages do something else too. They keep people out. They are boundaries that protect

the animals from the people."

"Would people really try to hurt animals?" Ollie asked.

"Some people would. Most people wouldn't hurt them on purpose, but they would feed them the wrong food or frighten them. So the cages are boundaries that protect the animals. People need boundaries too."

"You mean we should all live in cages?" Ollie asked with a laugh.

Mom laughed too. "Sometimes I think you should when I look at your room."

Dad shook his head. "We have taught you that your body is your own and that no one else has the right to touch it. You have the right to stop anything that makes you feel uncomfortable."

Ollie nodded.

"That's a boundary that you have. But every person also has the right to set boundaries around themselves that say, 'This is my space and my life. Stay back.' No one has the right to hurt you, to make you feel bad, or to make you change how you feel about yourself."

"But Herk does that," Ollie protested.

"We'll talk about what Herk does later. Let's think about what you're doing. This week, you've been moping around the house, not happy, not even playing soccer."

"But that's because of Herk."

"So you're letting Herk decide how you feel about yourself and whether or not you can play and have fun."

Ollie opened his mouth and then closed it. His dad was right.

"Oliver," his mom added, "you are the same special person you were last week. You're still smart, you're still a good soccer player, and you still have good friends."

Dad said, "You need to put up your boundaries that say, 'I'm in charge of how I feel about myself.' "

Ollie smiled. "I just need to put on my cage and take it with me. But what do I do about Herk?"

Dad stood up. "We'll work on a plan. Right now, it's feeding time for the sea lions. Let's go."

As Ollie walked off between his mom and dad, he felt happy. And he felt something else. For the first time that week, he was hungry. "OK, but let's hurry. I'm starving."

Standing Up to Herk

Class," Mrs. Appleby said, "it seems that some of us have forgotten how to treat one another. None of us has the right to hurt someone else, either by what we say or what we do."

Ollie felt his cheeks get a little red. *I wonder if Mom talked to her,* he thought.

"And remember," Mrs. Appleby went on, "if you purposely try to injure someone, you will be sent to the principal's office and probably suspended from school. Now, on a completely different subject, I want to announce that there will be an extra study session in math every day after school for those who are having trouble."

When she stepped out of the room later, kids began to whisper. One whisper wasn't very quiet. In fact, Ollie heard it all the way from the back of the room.

"He's not just a wimp. He's a tattletale too."

Ollie didn't have to turn around to know who said that. He

Setting boundaries;
dealing with hatred; self-esteem

thought about the plan he and his parents had worked out at the zoo. From now on, he was going to be in charge of how he felt. The plan for dealing with Herk started with ignoring him.

"Whatever he says, just ignore it," Dad had suggested. "If he wants to start an argument, just walk away. If he tries to hurt you, report it to the teacher. Don't let him decide how you will act."

At recess, Ollie joined the others on the soccer field. "All right," Derek said when he saw Ollie, "you're gonna play."

"What are you doing here, Polly?" Herk asked loudly. "You're too little to play this game."

Ollie just turned away and joined his team on their end of the field. All during the game, he kept running with the ball whenever it came near him. That way, he was never standing where Herk would want to kick the ball.

Once, he kicked the ball right past Herk's head. "Watch it, wimp," Herk yelled.

"Next time, hit him," Derek shouted from the goalie box. Ollie ignored both of them and kept playing the game. The next time Herk had the ball, Ollie dashed in from the side and kicked it away. Herk stopped and pointed at Ollie.

"You got lucky that time, Polly," he said. "Next time, I'll be kicking you instead of the ball." Ollie just kept running after the ball.

When recess was over, Ollie and Derek lined up with the others. Suddenly, Herk cut in front of them. "You just stay out of my way on the soccer field, Polly."

Ollie just turned his head and looked away. Herk shoved him back against the wall. "Hey, I'm talking to you, wimp."

"Herk!" Mr. Morrison called from the front of the line. "Please stay after school today. We need to talk."

"Ooooh," the guys in line said. "Someone's in trouble." Herk scowled and turned away.

After school, Ollie and Derek were back in the schoolyard, practicing soccer again. "Let me try a few more kicks with my left foot," Ollie called to Derek. This time, more of them were getting through to the net. He was concentrating so hard that he didn't notice that anyone else was around until a hand grabbed his shirt.

"Hey, Polly, you got me in trouble with Mr. Morrison today." Herk yanked Ollie around until their noses were almost touching. "And didn't I tell you to stay off this field after school?"

Ollie knew that ignoring Herk wasn't going to work. And he knew the next step in the plan. His dad had said, "If Herk still won't leave you alone, you'll have to stand up to him. Just

tell him that he's not in charge of you or the soccer field. He might hit you, but you have permission to defend yourself if necessary."

Ollie took a deep breath and thought a quick prayer, *God, help me be brave enough to hold up my cage walls.* Then he shoved Herk's hand off his shirt. "Look, you're not in charge of me or this field. Why don't you leave me alone?"

Herk growled. "Maybe I'll just leave you here in pieces."

Ollie swallowed. "You might. But if you do, I'll tell Mr. Morrison and my parents and your parents and the principal. And I'll keep telling them until you're in so much trouble, you'll never see recess again."

Derek stepped up beside him. "And if you want to start anything, you'll have to fight both of us."

Herk just looked at them for a second, then threw up his hands and walked away. "You're not worth the trouble."

Ollie let out a big breath he didn't even know he was holding. "Thanks, Derek, for standing up to him with me."

"No problem, buddy," Derek said. "But you didn't need me. You were standing up to him all by yourself. I don't know if I could do that."

"You just have to set your own boundaries," Ollie said. "I'm not going to let Herk or anyone else decide how I should feel every day. I'm in charge of that."

Derek looked surprised. "You've sure changed a lot since last week. Let's practice some more before I have to go."

The next day at school, the classroom was buzzing with news. As usual, Derek met Ollie at the door. "Hey, Ollie, everyone says that Mr. Morrison is going to let us play a real soccer game against the other-fifth grade room this Friday for P.E."

Standing Up to Herk

"Great," Ollie agreed. "Has anyone seen them play? Are they any good?"

"Well, their best player was Herk. But now he's on our team. It should be an easy win for us."

One of the other class soccer players, Janet, heard what Derek was saying. "Don't be so sure," she said. "Herk said that Mr. Morrison was going to let him play with his old class, since they have fewer kids."

Derek whistled. "That means you and I will have to play against him," he said to Ollie.

Ollie nodded. "It seems like it's always him against me."

Standing Up to Herk

Who Cares?

Well, how is it going at school this week, Oliver?" It was suppertime, and Ollie waited for the usual question. "What do you have to be thankful for today?"

"My troubles with Herk seem to be over for now," he said. "And I'm having fun playing soccer again."

His mom shook her head. "If you get any better at kicking, we'll have to be replacing those front steps soon." But she was smiling, and Ollie knew she was proud of him. "I'm glad your boundaries helped you deal with that bully."

"I'm glad that it's over."

Mom said, "It's not really over."

"What do you mean?"

"You learned how to deal with this bully and how to stand up for your rights. But someday, you need to take it one step farther. You need to change your enemy into a friend."

Ollie laughed. "Herk? A friend? I don't think so. He hates my guts."

**Setting boundaries;
dealing with hatred; self-esteem**

She smiled. "I'm sure he likes your intestines more than you think. Besides, the Bible tells you the secret of changing enemies into friends."

"What's the secret?"

"Surprise them with kindness. It works every time. Kindness and love are always stronger than hate."

Ollie didn't want to disappoint his mother, but this time, he was sure she was wrong. She would be surprised to know just how mean Herk was. And if the Bible really said that, then God would be surprised too.

The next afternoon, Ollie was nearly home when he jerked to a stop. "My math book!" he said out loud. "I left it in my desk."

On his way back out of the classroom, he stopped by the water fountain. While he was drinking, he heard Herk's voice

coming from the room next to it. "I don't care. No one likes me anyway."

Ollie listened as Mr. Morrison's voice drifted out into the hallway. "Herk, you can't treat other people any way you want to. They have a right to be treated fairly or left alone."

Herk's voice grew louder. "Hey, no one treats me fairly. Do you know what it's like living with a name like Herk? It's always 'Herk the Jerk,' or something."

"But don't you see," Mr. Morrison's voice went on, "if you treated other people with respect, they would do the same for you? You could make real friends. People who really like you for who you are."

Ollie heard Herk's snort. "I'll tell you who I really hate. Kids like that Ollie. They always try to make me look bad with their 'A' papers in math and everything. Well, I can show them a thing or two in soccer."

"I think if you really got to know some of the other kids in this room, you'd find out that they're a lot like you. They have the same kind of problems," Mr. Morrison said.

Ollie backed away from the water fountain, trying not to make any noise. Finally, he made it outside. Now he knew why Herk hated him. "But what am I supposed to do?" he asked himself out loud. "Fail math, too, so he'll be happy?"

The more he thought about it, the more he could under-stand why Herk acted like such a jerk. He had to live with all the teasing about his name, and he didn't do very well in school. *I wonder if anyone helps him at home like Mom helps me,* Ollie thought as he kicked his soccer ball down the street.

The next day, Herk wasn't at school. Some of the kids reported that he had gone back to his old class, but Mrs. Appleby said he was just home sick.

"I wish he would go back to his old class," Derek said at recess. "It's a lot quieter around here without him."

Ollie had to agree with that. And for once, he could play soccer and just think about the game, instead of wondering where Herk was and where he might come from next. It was a great recess.

But the next day, Herk was back. And Ollie's troubles with him continued.

On Thursday, the day before the big game, Derek had to go to the dentist. So Ollie practiced alone at the schoolyard after school. As much as he hoped it wouldn't happen, he wasn't surprised to hear Herk's voice behind him.

"What a wimp! Is that as hard as you can kick?"

Ollie just ignored him and pulled the ball out of the net. But Herk wasn't going away.

"Hey! I asked you a question." Herk grabbed him by his shirt again. "There's no Mr. Morrison around now to keep me from kicking you around the field. And your little buddy's not here either." He pulled Ollie's shirt tighter as he spoke.

Ollie coughed, but he looked Herk right in the eye. "You could do that. But it wouldn't change anything. I'd still tell the teachers. And I'd still be here tomorrow. It's my school and my schoolyard too."

Herk just stared at him.

Ollie added, "Why do you hate me anyway? I never call you Herk the Jerk or anything."

Herk let go of Ollie's shirt. "What makes you think I care what you call me, Polly? I don't care what you say. Or what anyone else says."

Ollie tried to uncrumble his bunched-up shirt. "Good," he said. "I don't care if you call me Polly either."

Herk stared at him again. "You are too weird." He started walking away but turned back to shout, "You just better be careful tomorrow in the big game. You might get hurt."

With a sigh, Ollie picked up his ball and headed for home. *So much for becoming friends,* he thought. *Are my troubles with Herk ever going to end?*

The Big Game

"Class. Class!" Mrs. Appleby had to raise her voice to get the kids settled. "I know you are all looking forward to the soccer game, but we do have to do our reading today too."

The morning crawled slowly by until, finally, it was time for P.E. "Kick me some practice shots," Derek called to Ollie as they gathered on the field.

Herk and his friends from the other class watched and laughed. "What a wimpy kick! Are you sure you guys aren't in fourth grade?"

Finally, Mr. Morrison arrived. He gathered the fifth-graders around. "This is going to be a real game, so we'll be playing according to all the rules of soccer you've been learning in P.E. Remember that you must throw the ball over your head when you bring it inbounds and that you must not kick at the ball if you've fallen to the ground. Everyone ready? Let's line up."

**Setting boundaries;
dealing with hatred; self-esteem**

The Big Game

3-G.S.K. ENGv4

Ollie started the game at halfback, helping Derek protect their goal. Herk was playing forward and kicked the ball right at Ollie every time he had the chance. But Ollie stepped fast and worked at stealing the ball away. The second time he stole the ball, Herk reached out and shoved him to the ground.

Pfeet! Mr. Morrison's whistle stopped play. "Herk, there is no pushing in the game of soccer. One more play like that, and you will be thrown out of the game. Free kick from here for Ollie's team."

Herk scowled as Ollie booted the ball toward the other goal. But he didn't do any more pushing. Both teams played hard, and no one scored until the last minute of the first half. Herk and another player on his team rushed up Ollie's side toward the goal.

Ollie made a move to steal the ball, just as the player kicked toward Herk. Herk and the ball moved right past Ollie. "Look out, Derek!" Ollie shouted.

But Herk's kick flew right past Derek's diving fingertips and into the net. "Yaay!" Herk shouted. "I knew we would beat these wimps."

"Sorry about that," Derek told his team as they sipped water at half time.

"It was my fault," Ollie said.

"It doesn't matter," Janet said. "But we need to score. How about you moving up to striker, Ollie. I'll move to halfback, and Mark moves to forward."

Ollie waited at center field to kick the ball and start the second half. He liked playing striker, because he could run the whole field, playing defense and offense.

But this half was much like the first one. Both teams played well, and neither one could score a goal. With only a

minute left, Ollie took the ball on a pass from Janet and started up the field. He passed it over to Mark and ran ahead of it toward the goal.

Mark made a perfect kick between two of their players, and the ball landed right at Ollie's feet. Only one person stood between him and the goalie. But that person was Herk!

"Go, Ollie," he heard Derek yell from the other end. Ollie raced forward, straight at Herk. Herk came straight at him, like he wasn't worried about Ollie at all.

Ollie turned like he was going around to Herk's left, as he usually did. Then, at the last second, he spun and went the other way, kicking the ball with his left foot.

Herk was faked off his feet. He ended up on the ground, and Ollie blew by. The goalie leapt, but Ollie's kick blasted the ball into the corner of the net. Before anyone could move, the whistle sounded the end of the game. They had tied, 1-1.

"All right!" "Great shot!" Ollie's team rushed at him and shouted as they pounded each other on the back.

"Good game," Mr. Morrison called to them. "Great shot, Ollie."

The other team wasn't as happy, but since no one lost, everyone felt pretty good. Everyone except Herk. Ollie watched as he walked away, alone.

The next week, Herk didn't play soccer so often at recess. And Ollie and Derek never saw him after school. Ollie was thinking about that when Mrs. Appleby announced another math test. Then he thought about what his mother had said about friends and enemies. That afternoon, he walked up to the teacher's desk. "Mrs. Appleby?"

"Yes, Oliver?"

"Could I stay for the math study session today?"

Mrs. Appleby looked at him over her glasses. "You don't usually need help with math, Oliver."

Ollie smiled. "I know. I thought I might help someone else."

"Well, that's a fine idea," she replied. "Certainly you could help. Just stay in this room after the bell."

When the classroom cleared out at the end of the day, only three other kids were left. Herk, as usual, was at the back of the room. Ollie took a deep breath and walked back to the desk beside Herk. As he slid in, he said, "Hi."

Herk looked up from his math book and frowned. "What are you doing here? I thought all you 'A' students went home."

Ollie opened his book. "Not today. I need to study for our test tomorrow."

"You? Study? I thought you were supposed to know it all," Herk said with a snort.

"No way," Ollie answered. "I have to study for every test too."

"Then why don't I ever see you here after school?"

Ollie smiled. "I usually study at home. My mom is real good at explaining math. Derek studies there with me a lot. But my mom is busy today, so I thought I would stay and study here."

Herk looked at him but didn't say anything.

Ollie tried smiling again. "Want to study together?"

"OK."

The next day at recess, Mr. Morrison picked Janet and Herk to be captains. "Herk, you pick first."

Herk looked around for a second. Then with a smile, he said, "I'll take Ollie."

No one was more surprised than Ollie.

TEN MILLION BILLION

Sarah, it's Friday. Don't forget your library book today."

"OK, Mom," Sarah answered. *I remember it,* she said to herself, *I just don't remember where it is.*

She sat down on her bed and tried to picture just where the book might be. *I finished reading it last Monday, so it should be on my bookshelf. But I know it isn't—I've been through those books three times.*

Maybe it fell under my bed. She dropped to her knees and pulled up the bedspread. There was a barrette, one red sock, and some old school papers, but no book. *Maybe it's still in my book bag, under my spelling book and stuff.* But inside, she only found school books and papers.

Prayer; God's power

"Sarah, Maggie, let's go. I don't want to be late."

All the way to the day-care center, Maggie talked nonstop. Sarah kept very quiet. *Maybe Mom won't ask about the book. Maybe it's in my desk at school.*

Mom didn't ask, but the book wasn't there. And when her mother arrived to pick her up after school, it was the first thing she asked about.

"Are we ready to go to the library?"

"No. I couldn't find my book. I've looked everywhere," Sarah wailed.

Her mother wasn't happy either. "Sarah, you know you'll have to pay the fine for a late book yourself."

"I know, I know. I just can't remember where I put it! Now, I'll probably have to pay for a new one."

Maggie reached up and patted Sarah's shoulder. "That's OK, Sarah. You can have one of my books."

Sarah smiled grimly. "Thanks."

Mom said, "Have you prayed and asked God to help you?"

"No," Sarah admitted. And inside, she wasn't sure she should. *God doesn't care about things like lost library books.*

Sarah looked through her room again, but the book was nowhere to be found. *I give up*, she decided. But at church that weekend, something made her think again.

"Class, this morning we have a special visitor," Sarah's teacher said. "Professor Benson is going to show us the stars."

Professor Benson laughed. "I can't show you all the stars, but I want you to see some of the amazing things God created out in space."

Sarah watched as Professor Benson showed them the planets. Then she told them how big the universe is. "If you could travel at the speed that light travels, you would move at 186,000 miles a second. If you could move that fast, you could speed all the way around the world seven times before I can say the words 'in a second.' "

"Whoa," someone said.

Professor Benson laughed. "So, if you could move that fast, it would still take more than six minutes to travel from the earth to the sun. How long do you think it would take to travel across the whole universe that God created?"

No one would even guess.

"It would take twenty billion years."

Wow, Sarah thought, *if God is that powerful, then maybe He could help me find my book. Maybe He would if I asked Him.*

Then someone asked, "If the universe is that big, how many worlds are there like ours?"

Professor Benson answered, "In our galaxy—our part of

Kevin Merrell

the universe—there are 200 billion suns like ours. And there are 100 billion other galaxies like ours. So there may be as many as ten million billion planets in this universe."

Sarah slumped in her chair. *With that many places to lose things, I'm sure God doesn't have time to be bothered with my library book.*

By Sunday afternoon, Mom got serious about the lost book. "It's a good reason for you to clean your room from top to bottom. Straighten out that bookshelf, make your bed, and put away your toys. You might find the book right under your nose."

For once, Sarah liked the idea of cleaning her room. She got so carried away cleaning that she forgot all about the book. When everything was in its place, she stopped and looked around. *Hey, this is nice*, she decided with a smile. Then she remembered. *I still didn't find the book.*

"You'll have to look through the rest of the house," her mother decided. So Sarah searched through the bookshelves in the living room and through the toy box in Maggie's room.

"It's just not here, Mom," she reported.

"Have you asked God to help you find it?" her mother asked.

"Come on, Mom," Sarah said with a laugh. "God is too busy to keep track of little things like that. Do you know how many places He has to look?"

Mom smiled. "I guess I don't. But I do know that He cares. Even about the little things. Sarah, the Bible says that God even keeps track of how many hairs are on our heads."

Sarah felt her head. "That's another ten million things to keep track of."

"He loves you, Sarah, ten million billion times more than

you can imagine. Ask for His help, and maybe the book will show up where you least expect it."

Sarah went back to her room. "God," she said out loud, "if You're not too busy, will You help me find my library book? I'll keep looking, but I'm running out of ideas. It's OK if You don't—it's my fault that it's lost. Thanks for loving me so much. Amen."

Sarah searched the car and then the garage. She was going through the laundry room—in case the book had been thrown into her dirty clothes hamper—when she heard a voice from the kitchen.

"Sarah, would you put Maggie to bed and read her a story?"

I'm busy looking for my book, she started to say. But she didn't. *I really don't have anywhere else to look.* "OK, Mom."

By the time she finished reading Maggie's story, Sarah decided that she didn't feel so bad about the missing book. *It'll be OK,* she decided, *even if I don't find it before tomorrow.*

"Hey," she said to Maggie as she tucked in the covers, "what is this doll doing in your bed?" Maggie just giggled. Sarah reached farther back under the covers. "And what about this plastic lizard?"

Maggie giggled again. "I hide my toys there so I'll have something to play with if I wake up in the dark," she explained.

Sarah laughed. "You don't wake up to play, silly. You sleep all night." She reached back under the covers and pulled out one more thing. A book. Her missing library book!

"Maggie, you had my book!"

"I liked the pictures," Maggie said in a sleepy voice.

Sarah's mouth hung open. "But—I . . ." Finally, she just turned out the light and sat there, thinking about lost books and millions and billions of other things.

Finally, Sarah stood up. "Thank You, God," she whispered. Then she ran down the hall to show her mother.

A Stranger at the Door

Briinng!

Philip didn't move from his spot on the couch. "Telephone!" he shouted. Then he remembered. *There's no one home but me.*

Briinng! Philip bounced up and grabbed the phone. "Hello."

"Hi, is your dad there?" a man asked.

"No."

"Not home from work yet, huh. I guess that leaves you there all alone, doesn't it?"

The man talked like someone that Philip should know, but Philip didn't recognize the voice. "Yeah, I guess so. Do you want to leave a message?"

"No, I'll call again later. 'Bye."

Philip went back to the couch and the TV. *Rats. I missed the end of my show. And there's nothing on but the boring news.* Still, Philip sat and watched.

Protection from strangers

Ding-dong. Now who could that be? Philip
wondered as he hopped up again. He took a second to look
through the peephole. A man wearing a blue uniform was
there. *Must be delivering something,* Philip decided as he
opened the door.

"Hi," the man said. "Is one of your parents home?"

Philip shook his head. "Just me. Did we get a package?"

"Yeah," the man said, looking at his clipboard. "But an
adult needs to sign for it. I'll come back." With that, he left.

Why are these people bothering me this afternoon? Philip

asked as he sat back down. Then the news reporter got his attention.

"Are you home alone tonight?"

Why does everyone keep asking that? Philip wondered.

"Many children watching tonight would have to answer *Yes.* And the sad truth is, a child left alone is the one most likely to be targeted by a child molester or kidnapper."

"Whoa," Philip said. "Not me."

"Here in our studio this week, we'll be talking to Officer Perez of the City Police. Officer Perez has taken a leading role in educating our community about the dangers to children. He visits our schools to teach children how to protect themselves. Officer Perez, what can we do to protect the children?"

The camera switched to a young police officer. "What we can do is teach all children about safety. Not the kind of safety that means looking both ways before crossing the street but the kind that has to do with protecting yourself from strangers."

"Oh yeah, right," Philip mumbled. "Like someone's going to kidnap me on the way home." He rolled his eyes.

"How do criminals find their victims?" the reporter asked.

"They look for a child who is alone. Often, this is at the child's home. It's important for kids to be safe on the phone. They should never admit to any stranger that they're home alone."

Philip's face got red. "I wonder who I talked to on the phone? Did he really know Dad?"

Officer Perez smiled at the camera. "If you are home alone and you answer the phone, say something like, 'My dad can't come to the phone right now. Can I take a message?' You don't have to say that your father or mother isn't there with

A Stranger at the Door

you. It's none of the caller's business where your parents are."

Philip started to feel a little nervous. Then Officer Perez said, "Kids, if you are home alone, never answer the doorbell. Whoever it is will come back later. Even if someone has figured out that you're alone, you're still safe with your doors locked."

Now Philip felt a lot more nervous. "I told a stranger on the phone that I was home alone. Then I opened the door to a stranger and told him that no adults were here. And that delivery guy said he would be back. If he really was a delivery guy!"

The TV news kept going. Officer Perez said, "If you do feel threatened or afraid of someone, your best defense is to make as much noise as possible. Scream, shout, jump up and down, do anything to get attention. That's the last thing a criminal wants, and he'll usually run away."

The camera cut back to the reporter. "We'll continue our talk with Officer Perez tomorrow. The weather forecast is next."

Philip got up and peered through the door again. "I've got to do something," he said. "This guy already knows I'm here

alone. He may come back soon and break the door in." Philip thought about what the officer had said. Then he came up with a plan. Before long, he crawled under the table with the stereo remote control in his hand. A few seconds later, he heard a noise at the door. He closed his eyes. "I hope this works."

The door opened slowly and quietly. Until it hit the string holding the pots and pans up. *Crash! Boom! Bam!* When they fell onto the cookie tins, it sounded like the inside of a thunderstorm. Then Philip hit a button on the remote.

Woo-woo-woo! The sound of the police siren was so loud it almost peeled the paint off the walls.

Finally, Philip looked up to see if the stranger was gone. "Oops," he said. It wasn't a stranger. It was his dad.

"What in the . . . Philip!" Dad bellowed while rubbing his head with one hand and covering his ear with the other. Philip crawled out to try and explain.

"I can't hear you," his dad shouted. "Turn that noise off!"

"Calling all cars. Calling all cars," the stereo screamed. Philip hit the right button, and it stopped.

"I'm sorry, Dad. I thought you were a stranger trying to break in." Philip explained about the phone call and the delivery guy. "The police officer on TV said a kid should never do what I did."

"Hey," a voice from the door said. "Is everything OK in here?" It was the delivery guy.

"Yes, it's fine," Dad said, signing the paper. "Just a little problem with the stereo." He kicked a pan out of the way. "And the dishwasher."

As the delivery guy left, the phone rang. Dad picked it up. "Hello? Oh, hi, Tom. Yes, he mentioned that someone called for me. OK, we'll deal with it tomorrow."

By now, Philip was wishing he could crawl back under the table. "I guess I was really stupid," he said when his dad hung up. "There was no dangerous stranger after all."

Dad shook his head. "Ow," he said, rubbing it again. "No, Philip, you're not stupid. It wasn't a criminal this time. But it might be next time. I want you to remember how to keep next time from happening. I'll take a knock on the noggin every day if that means you'll be safe."

Philip's face broke into a smile. "Thanks, Dad."

HOW TO BE SAFE FROM STRANGERS

1. Never tell a stranger on the phone that you are alone.
2. Say, "My mom can't come to the phone now. Can I take a message?"
3. If someone has a wrong number, never tell them yours. Just say,"I'm sorry, you have the wrong number," and hang up.
4. Never answer the doorbell if you're alone. If it's important, the person will come back later when an adult is home.
5. Call the police or 9-1-1 if someone is trying to break into your house.
6. If a person is threatening you or scaring you, scream, shout, and make as much noise as possible.

A Stranger in the Park

T here he goes!" Laurelle shouted. "Don't let him get to that tree!" Chasing her friend Kelsey and a squirrel through the park's trees was more fun than swinging. The park squirrel was used to kids by now. It sat calmly until Kelsey was only a step away. Then, with a flick of its tail, it flashed up the tree. *Chit-chit-chit!* Sitting just above their reach, the squirrel gave the girls the scolding they deserved.

"He always gets away," Laurelle complained. On the street next to the park, a man leaning against his car laughed.

"Hey, girls," the man called, "come here, and I'll give you some peanuts. Then maybe you can catch him."

Laurelle looked at her friend. "I'd better go," Kelsey said. "Mom said to be home before supper. See you tomorrow."

"No, thanks," Laurelle called to the man. Then she walked home slowly, kicking leaves across the park.

"Supper will be ready soon," her mom said when she came in. "Will you fold the clothes on the couch before we eat?"

Protection from strangers

Laurelle clicked on the TV as she sat down. "Nothing but news," she grumbled. But she left it on anyway.

A reporter was talking. "This is the second part of our interview with Officer Perez of the City Police. Officer Perez often visits our schools to teach children how to protect themselves from strangers. Officer Perez, last night we talked about ways kids can protect themselves at home. What can kids do to keep safe when they're out playing or walking to school?"

The camera switched to a young police officer. "Kids have

heard a lot about being safe, looking both ways before crossing the street, and wearing visible clothes at night. But they don't hear enough about protecting themselves from strangers."

Laurelle shook out a towel and rolled her eyes. *Like someone's going to kidnap me right in the park.*

"How do these criminals find their young victims?" the reporter asked.

"First, they usually find a child who is alone. Kids who walk home from school or from the park alone are just the kind of target they look for."

Laurelle put the towel down. *I've never seen any dangerous-looking people.* She kept listening.

Officer Perez said, "Whether you're alone or with a friend, remember that you should never get in the car with someone you don't know—no matter what they tell you. Some kids have heard, 'Your mom told me to pick you up,' or 'I'll give you a ride home.' Don't do it. Also, be suspicious of any adult who asks a child for help, like asking for directions. Adults who really need help or directions will ask another adult, not a kid."

Laurelle started to feel a little nervous. *What about that guy who offered us peanuts? I wonder if he was dangerous?*

Then Officer Perez said, "Kids, if someone talks to you from their car, you don't have to answer. I know it seems rude, but some adults take advantage of kids who are being polite. And if anyone invites you over to their car to see something, just leave. Find an adult you trust, and tell them what happened."

Now Laurelle felt a lot more nervous. *That's exactly what that guy wanted us to do! I'd better tell Kelsey about this.*

A Stranger in the Park

The TV news kept going. "Kids," Officer Perez said, "if you do feel threatened or afraid of someone, your best defense is to make as much noise as possible. Scream, shout, jump up and down, do anything to get attention. That's the last thing a criminal wants, and he'll usually run away."

The camera cut back to the reporter. "Thanks, Officer Perez. Will it rain tomorrow? The weather forecast is next."

The next day, Laurelle met Kelsey in the park again, and they spent a half-hour on the swings. "Whoa, I'm starting to get sick," Kelsey said. "Let's rest for a while."

As they coasted back and forth, a man wearing a brown hat walked by. "Brownie!" he called. He shook the leash in his hand to make it jingle. "Come on, Brownie!" He turned toward Laurelle and Kelsey. "Have you seen a brown dog with one white paw?" he asked. "I lost my dog."

Before the girls could say anything, he asked, "Could I hire you two to help me look for Brownie? I'll pay you a dollar each if you'll search the park."

"Sure," Kelsey said. "We can help." They both jumped off the swings and went over to the man. He reached into his pocket and handed them each a dollar bill.

"Thanks. I'll drive around the block a few times, then meet you at the other end of the park."

"This is great," Kelsey said as the man walked away. "We get a dollar just for looking for a dog."

But as the man got into his car, something tickled the back of Laurelle's brain. "Kelsey, is that the same man we saw yesterday? The one with the peanuts?"

"I don't know," Kelsey said. "Why?"

"It looks like the same car to me," Laurelle said. Then she remembered what Officer Perez had said on the news. "Kelsey! On the news last night, a police officer said that one of the ways strangers trap children is by asking them for help."

"What?"

"Come on, Kelsey. Think about it. Why would he ask us to find his dog? He doesn't know us. Besides, adults don't usually ask kids for help. What if he's trying to trap us at the other end of the park? Where we'd be all alone?"

Kelsey's eyes got big. She dropped the dollar bill on the ground. "Laurelle, I'm scared. What should we do?"

Laurelle thought. "The police officer said that if a stranger tried to talk to you or asked you to come to their car, you should leave and find an adult to tell."

"Then let's go," Kelsey said. They hadn't gone far when Laurelle held out her hand.

"Wait! Look!"

"It's not him, is it?" Kelsey cowered behind her friend.

"No, it's a police car. Come on." Laurelle knocked on the car window. "A man in the park gave us money to help him find his dog. I saw the news last night, and that officer said that a man asking children for help could be dangerous."

"You did the right thing, girls," the officer said. "I'll go check him out. What did he look like?"

Later that night, Laurelle told her mom all about it. "I'm

A Stranger in the Park

sure glad Kelsey was with me," she added.

"So am I," her mom agreed. "Whether that man was a criminal or not, you did the right thing. Promise me you'll always be careful about strangers."

"I will."

HOW TO BE SAFE FROM STRANGERS

1. Never get into a stranger's car, no matter what they tell you.
2. Never go near a car with someone sitting in it or talk to a stranger in a car. Ignore them, or leave the scene.
3. Normal adults don't ask children for help or for directions. Ignore them or leave.
4. Report any adult who:
   - asks you to keep a secret.
   - wants to take your picture.
   - wants to give you gifts.
   - talks to you about love or sex.
5. Never go into someone else's home without your parents' permission.
6. If a person is threatening you or scaring you, scream, shout, and make as much noise as possible.

WORLD WAR FIVE

"Get out of our room, and stay out! I hate both of you!" Grant winced as the door slammed, but he wasn't surprised. The arguing that had gone on all morning was turning into a fight. And with steady rain falling outside, it looked as if there was no escape.

It's a beautiful day to lie on the couch and read a book, Grant thought as he tried to do just that. *If a person could hear himself think over all the noise!*

Being the older brother to two sets of twins meant that Grant was usually overlooked. People seemed fascinated by the twins. And since they each had each other to play with, Grant usually played alone.

Not that Grant minded much. He didn't like to be fussed over the way the twins were. And he did like being alone. Mostly because he liked the one thing he hadn't had all day. Quiet!

Why does it have to rain the one week Mom is working? he

Getting along with siblings; fighting fair

moaned. *I could send half of them outside if it wasn't.*

With thundering footsteps, Tommy and Timmy raced in and ducked down behind the couch. "This'll show who's the smartest."

"What did you guys do now?" Grant asked without looking up.

"Oh, nothing, really," Timmy answered with a snicker. "Just started World War Three."

"You mean World War Four," Tommy corrected. "World War Three was yesterday when we blasted them with our squirt guns."

Grant tried to read faster. He knew he only had a few seconds. And he was right. "Grant!" both girls shouted as they came in. "They stole our diary!"

"It's personal and private," Andrea said. "Make them give it back! Without reading it."

"How do you know we haven't read it already?" Timmy asked, popping up.

Grant wearily put his book down. "Guys, you wouldn't want anyone to read your private things."

Tommy popped up too. "We don't write private things down."

"Grant, make them give it back," Angela demanded.

"All right, just give me a minute," Grant said. As the two girls stomped away, he held out his hand. "OK, cough it up."

"Aw, come on, Grant," Timmy said. "We're just teasing them. We aren't going to read it or anything."

Just then, a paper airplane came coasting into the room. Timmy grabbed it. A message was printed on the wings in big letters: *HOSTAGE—ONE HAMSTER: RANSOM—ONE DIARY*

"They stole Huey! This means World War Five. Come on. Let's get him back!"

Grant closed his eyes and shook his head. "All I want is some peace and quiet," he mumbled. After a few seconds of pounding and shouting, he snapped.

"Timmy! Tommy! Get in here! Go sit at the table. Now!" They went, but not without dark glares at their brother. "Angela! Andrea! Get out here!" Their door slowly opened. "Go sit at the table," he demanded before they could start whining.

With the twins sitting on two sides of the table, Grant stood at the end. "If this is a war, then we'll have to settle it the way all wars should be settled."

"Fight to the death?" Timmy asked. "Cool!"

"No," Grant said. "A truce and negotiations. First, you agree to stop fighting and talk. Then you discuss how to stop the fighting for good."

Angela folded her arms and frowned. "You can't make us talk. Or stop fighting."

Grant nodded. "But Mom did say that I could decide whether or not to take you swimming tomorrow. So . . ."

Angela looked at Andrea. Timmy looked at Tommy. "OK," they all said.

"Good. Now, the first problem is a prisoner-of-war exchange. Timmy, do you agree to return the diary in exchange for Huey?"

Timmy glared at the girls. "OK."

"Girls? Do you agree?" They both nodded.

"Now," Grant said, "I asked Mom once why the four of you are always either fighting or playing together. She said that brothers and sisters sometimes fight because it's safe."

"What does that mean?" Tommy asked.

"If you fight with a friend, they might stop being your friend. But your sisters or brothers can't stop being your sisters or brothers even if you do fight."

"Too bad," Angela mumbled.

Grant frowned at her. "She also said that sometimes people fight because they're together too much. Especially on days like today, when they can't even go outside. That's why I'm trying to help instead of locking you in your rooms." He

paused to glare at each one. "Now, we'll make a list of grievances—that's all the things that make you fight. Andrea?"

Andrea pushed her lips out. "Those boys are always getting into our things. That starts the fighting."

"What do you mean?" Timmy shouted. "You're always in our room, digging around for stuff."

"That's where you hide what you take from us," Angela insisted. "We have to."

Grant waved his arms. "OK, OK. So you both want others to leave your things alone. See, you agree. I'll write it down."

As Grant kept them talking, the twins also agreed that they didn't like to be teased or embarrassed. "I don't like it when you say you hate me," Tommy said quietly.

Andrea's eyes dropped. "I don't really mean it. I just get mad. Especially when you say we're ugly or stupid."

"I don't really mean that either," Tommy admitted.

"Let's make a list of rules about fighting," Grant said.

"Number one, don't say things just to hurt the other person's feelings."

"Number two," Angela said, "no hitting or shoving or hurting someone."

"Number three," Timmy added, "no breaking or hurting their things—or their pets."

"Now," Grant said, "it's time for the prisoner exchange. That will seal our armistice—our plan for peace."

With the hamster and diary back in the right hands, the inside of the house seemed a lot cheerier. Suddenly, so did the outside. "Look!" Timmy said, "the rain stopped. Come on. Let's go see how deep the puddles are."

"Wait for us," Angela and Andrea called.

Grant went back to the couch and picked up his book. Finally, it was quiet. But before he got to the bottom of the first page, he heard Angela's voice from outside.

"You can't tell us what to do. This is our yard."

Then Tommy's voice. "Leave our sisters alone. Play in your own puddles."

Grant put his book down and headed for the door. "Sounds like World War Six. At least this time, they're on the same side."

Trouble on a Two-way Street

O h, please. Oh, please. Oh, please. Oh, please!"

Erin loved to roller-skate. She would do almost anything to go skating. Even beg, like she was doing now.

"We won't be gone long, and Cindy's mother will take us."

Her mother listened with a kind of frown on her face. Then she said, "If you'll hush for just a minute so I can think . . ."

Erin zipped her lips. She really did want to go. She had never been to the Roller Palace to skate. In fact, she had never been skating with Cindy at all. Cindy lived down the street. They played together sometimes, but they weren't really good friends.

"Erin, I don't know Cindy's mother very well. Are you sure she wants to take you?"

"Mom, I was there when Cindy asked her. She'll drop us off for two hours while she is shopping. Can I go?"

"I'm not sure I like you going to the Roller Palace. Can I trust you?"

Keeping promises; being trustworthy;
handling peer pressure

Erin rolled her eyes. She could have repeated what her mom was going to say next from memory.

"Trust is a two-way street, you know. Sometimes I have to trust you to do what's right. Sometimes, you have to trust me to know what's best—even when you don't understand why."

Here we go again, Erin thought. *What am I, a little kid? I know how to take care of myself!* "Yes, Mom. You can trust me."

Mom gave her a long stare. "OK. If Cindy's mother is taking you, I guess you can go. But, Erin . . ." She was talking to Erin's back now. Erin was busy digging in her closet for her skates with the neon green wheels. "Erin!"

"Yes, Mom?" Erin popped out with a skate in each hand.

"I don't want you to go outside of the skating rink. You go straight in to skate. When you're finished, wait inside until Cindy's mom stops to pick you up. OK?"

"OK, Mom. I promise." Erin didn't know what her mother was worried about. *I'd wait standing on my head if I had to. I just want to roller-skate!*

The rink was crowded with laughing, shouting, screaming kids. Erin zipped around with the others, flashing around the beginners and racing the faster kids. When they announced skating for couples, she went to the side for a drink.

"Look out!" Cindy shouted as Erin flew up to her and some of her friends. And Erin turned and stopped, just like she planned. "You're a great skater, Erin," Cindy said.

"I skate a lot," Erin said with a smile. "It's my favorite thing to do." She saw one of Cindy's friends roll his eyes like he thought she was crazy. She ignored him. "Do they ever do speed-skate racing here?"

"I think it's tomorrow night," Cindy said.

"Let's go," another girl standing nearby said. Erin noticed that Cindy's friends weren't even wearing skates. "Are you coming, Cindy?"

They looked at Cindy, and Cindy looked at Erin. "Do you want to go across the street and get some ice cream or something?" Cindy asked.

Erin looked at Cindy's friends. They were older kids, maybe sixth- or seventh-graders. Ice cream sounded good, but not when she could be skating. "No, I'd rather skate. Come on, Cindy. I'll race you around." Then she turned and took off without waiting for an answer.

Erin was halfway around the rink when Cindy cut across and skated up to her. "Thanks for helping me out there," she shouted over the noise of the skaters.

"What?" Erin asked. "What did I do?" They swerved to miss a pileup of little kids.

"You gave me a good reason not to go with them." They sped around a couple who were too busy holding hands to skate straight.

"Why didn't you want to go with them?" Erin asked.

"They're older than I am, and sometimes they get in trouble. My mom doesn't like them at all. If she knew they hung around here, she wouldn't even let me skate at this rink."

Erin shook her head. "Then why are they your friends?"

"I don't know," Cindy said. "They're just cool, I guess."

Near the end of their two hours, Cindy and Erin sat down to take off their skates. "Whoa." Erin wobbled as she stood up in her shoes. "I always have trouble remembering how to walk again."

"Let's go get a drink at the ice-cream shop," Cindy suggested as she tied her shoelaces.

"Sure," Erin said, and they headed for the door. Suddenly, she remembered her promise. *I'm old enough to wait across the street,* she argued with herself. *I know I promised, but Mom will never know.* Then she stopped and took a deep breath. *What if Mom really does know best?* "Wait, Cindy. I think I'll stay here."

"Why?"

"I promised my mom that I'd wait for your mother inside the skating rink."

"So? We'll just wait for her over there. It's no big deal," Cindy said as she held the door open. "You coming?"

Erin put her hand on the door, but then she stopped. "No, I'll wait here. I told her I would."

Cindy shrugged her shoulders and turned to cross the parking lot. Suddenly, a police car flashed around the corner and skidded to a stop right in front of the ice-cream shop. Two kids inside raced out the door and took off down the street. The officers leapt out of their car and chased after them. A second police car pulled up beside the first.

Cindy jumped back inside. "Did you see that?" she gasped.

"Weren't those your friends?"

Cindy just nodded and stared down the street. Her mother pulled up but stopped to talk to the police officer in the second car. When she drove to the front of the skating rink door, Erin and Cindy jumped in.

Trouble on a Two-way Street

"Can you believe that?" Cindy's mom asked, pointing to the police car. "Right here in front of the skating rink, kids are selling drugs! You're not skating here ever again, Cindy. Sorry about this, Erin."

At home, Erin went straight to her mother and hugged her tight. "Am I ever glad I listened to you, Mom. You were right." She told her about Cindy's friends and the police.

"Mom, I told myself that you would never know if I kept my promise. But you would have. You probably would have seen me on the news! Or at the police station."

Her mother just shook her head and smiled. "I knew I could trust you."

Erin grinned back. "It's a two-way street. I knew I could trust you too."

Fake Super Scout

11

"Now can we go, Dad?" Kyle dropped the last load of wood by the campfire bowl. We've got a lot of exploring to do."

Kyle's dad took a look at his list. "Did we get the lanterns out of the truck?"

"Check," Kyle answered.

"Did we get the tent stakes pounded in?"

"Check!" Rikki called from behind a tent. "Mom and I just finished."

"Hmmm." Dad thought for a second. "Mom, what else needs to be done?" he called.

Mom shouted back, "Kyle, did you get water for lunch?"

"Oops. I'll go get that now." He grabbed the water jug and ran to the camp faucet.

Finally, Dad agreed that everything was done. "You're going to see if the Richardsons' kids can go, aren't you?"

"Of course, Dad!" Kyle halted in midrun. "They're prob-

**Living with your conscience;
dealing with emergencies**

ably waiting for us."

"OK, but be careful. And don't go too far. It would be easy to get lost up here."

Kyle patted his backpack. "Don't worry. I've got everything we need right here."

According to Kyle and Rikki, the only thing better than camping was camping in a place they had never been before. And this was their first trip to Buffalo Mountain. The whole place needed to be explored.

Finally, they thundered into the Richardsons' camp. "Aaron! Sasha! Are you ready to go?" Kyle called. "I saw a creek down that hill. Let's go check it out."

"I'm right behind you!" Aaron answered.

"Be careful," Mrs. Richardson called.

"The last one to the creek is a rotten egg!"

Kyle and Aaron turned and raced through the trees toward the little creek at the bottom of the hill. Rikki and Sasha followed along more slowly, ignoring the boys' race. "This place is great," Sasha said. "Dad said it rains up here a lot in the summer, but I don't see a cloud in the sky."

By the time they got to the creek, the boys were wet up to their ankles. "Let's not get wet yet," Rikki suggested. "Let's keep going and explore the woods. We can come back to the creek to play later."

"OK," Kyle agreed, racing to a big rock in the middle of the meadow. "I'll be the lookout." Then he froze. "Shh! I think I see something!"

The others stopped in their tracks.

"It's a deer," Kyle reported. "It's moving toward the woods."

"Let me see," Aaron whispered, clambering up on the rock. "Where?"

"We want to see too," the girls insisted. By the time everyone was up there, the deer was gone.

"Come on. Let's try to track it." Kyle hopped down and started across the meadow. But by the time they had crossed through a stand of trees and into another meadow, the deer was forgotten.

"Hey, Aaron," Kyle whispered, "let's play a trick on the girls. Let's tell them we're lost."

Aaron looked around. "Are we lost? I don't know which way camp is."

Kyle pointed to a tree that was sticking up higher than any others. "See that tree? That's the big one just down from our campsite. As long as we can see that, we know the way home. Come on. It'll be fun."

They walked along through the meadow a little farther. Then Kyle stopped. "Wait a minute," he said loudly. "Where are we?"

Rikki looked at him. "What do you mean? We're at Buffalo Mountain."

Kyle rolled his eyes. "I know that. But where's our campground?" He tried to look scared. "I think we're lost."

Sasha looked annoyed. "Let's just go back the way we came." She turned and looked around. "Which way was that?"

Rikki pointed behind them. "It's that way. Come on." Kyle and Aaron followed the girls as they wound back across the meadow. "This is the way," Rikki repeated. "Remember that slanted tree next to that rock?"

"No," Kyle said. "I don't."

"I don't either," Sasha said. "We really are lost!"

Rikki looked a little worried too. "Let's just keep going this way. We'll see something we recognize soon." They kept going, wandering through a meadow and then some woods and then a meadow again. Every time they were out in the open, Kyle kept an eye on the big tree.

"We're still going the wrong way," Aaron snickered as they lagged behind the girls. "And they're really starting to get worried."

"Look," Sasha called, "there's the creek. We're almost back to camp!" They ran toward the shiny ribbon of water and collapsed at the bank.

"This isn't the right creek," Rikki wailed. "There's no hill to climb toward camp. There's no camp!"

For a second, Kyle thought she was going to cry. *I'd better get us back,* he decided. "Wait a minute," he said out loud. "Let me check something out." He dropped his backpack and pulled out a compass. "Let's see, north is that way." He licked his finger and held it up in the air. "The wind is from the southwest. Aaron, wasn't the wind blowing from the southeast when we left camp?"

Aaron tried to sound serious. "Yes, that's right."

Kyle wandered downstream. Then he stopped. "The camp is that way," he announced, pointing directly toward the big tree. "Let's go."

"Are you sure?" Sasha asked.

Kyle just smiled and strapped on his backpack. "That's where I'm going." He sniffed loudly. "Besides, can't you smell lunch cooking?"

After cutting across the side of the mountain, they came to another stream. And on the hill above it, they saw the smoke of a campfire. "See, there it is!"

"All right!" Rikki yelled. She and Sasha raced ahead, up the hill.

"They never even suspected," Kyle bragged. "Now they'll think we're the best scouts in the forest."

By the time the girls finished bragging about Kyle to their parents, even Kyle was embarrassed. "He knew exactly how to figure out the way home," Sasha said. "I won't be worried about being lost with him around."

Aaron sounded like he was choking on his beans. "Are you OK, dear?" his mother asked.

"Kyle, will you show us how to do that thing with your compass and the wind?" Rikki asked.

Now Kyle was feeling guilty. He turned away and helped himself to some more bread. "Just follow your nose, I always say," he answered. "Mom, are there any more beans?"

They rested around camp and played some games most of the afternoon. Finally, they decided it was time for more exploring. "Let's go back down to the creek," Aaron suggested.

"Yeah, let's go," Rikki added. "Mom, can we?"

"I guess so," she answered. "But don't go far. It gets dark quickly when the sun goes down behind the mountain."

"Whoop!" Kyle shouted as he raced back down the hill. This time, everyone raced after him. "Let's build a dam in the creek and see if we can make a pool big enough to swim in."

With their shoes off, the girls waded in and started moving rocks into a line across the narrow stream. Kyle and Aaron disappeared upstream. "Rikki, help me move this big one," Sasha called as she bent over a rock as big as a volleyball.

The mud squished between their toes as they lifted. Suddenly, something jumped from the rock right onto Sasha's arm. She screamed and dropped the rock, but she didn't see anything on her arm. "What was that?"

Attack of the Frogs

12

What was what?" Rikki started to ask. Then something jumped on her leg. "Yikes!" She brushed at her leg and backed off to where Sasha stood.

"What's going on?" Their shouting brought Kyle and Aaron running back. "What's all the shouting about?" Kyle asked.

Rikki pointed to the water. "Something is in there. Something that jumps."

Aaron waded out into the water. "Where is it?" he asked. "It's probably just a bug or something," he added as he lifted a rock. "Did you see where it went?"

"We didn't see it at all," Sasha said. "We just felt it land on us."

Kyle joined Aaron in the water. He saw something, then bent down to see it more closely. "Aaron, look. Is that a tiny frog?" Just then, it jumped, and both boys jumped back.

"It was a frog!" Aaron answered. "Look, here's another

**Living with your conscience;
dealing with emergencies**

one." He reached for it, but before his hands got there, it jumped—right onto his leg. Quick as a wink, it crawled up inside his shorts.

Suddenly, Aaron was the one doing the jumping. "Whoa! Hey! Aii!" He hopped right up onto the bank.

"What happened?" Sasha shouted. Kyle was laughing too hard to answer.

"Whoa!" Aaron shouted again. Then he hopped over behind some bushes.

"What's wrong?" Rikki asked. Kyle tried to stop laughing. "It's a little frog—and it jumped up his shorts!"

Everyone was still laughing when Aaron reappeared. "It got away," he said with a red face.

"Look," Kyle called, "there are lots of them—tiny little frogs."

"Let's catch one to show Dad," Rikki said, and they all joined the search. Laughing, jumping, and shouting, they ran from rock to rock, trying to grab the leaping frogs. Each little pond in the stream held more frogs, and they splashed their way upstream, racing past each other to get to the next frogs first.

"I've got one," Aaron shouted. "It's trapped on this rock. Kyle, give me your flashlight!"

Kyle reached for his backpack, but it wasn't there. "I didn't bring my backpack. If it wasn't so dark, we could have caught a bunch of them."

It struck all of them at once. "Hey, when did it get so

dark?" Rikki asked with a shiver. "And cold?"

"It's drizzling," Aaron complained. "Where did that come from?" The last glow of daylight shone through a bank of clouds and fog. "Wow, that was quick."

"Where are we?" Sasha asked in a small voice. The woods around them seemed to be getting darker by the second.

Rikki looked at Kyle. "It's a good thing you're here, Kyle. How do we get back to the campground?"

Kyle swallowed hard and looked around at the growing darkness. There was no way he could see the tall tree now. "Well, uh . . ." He could see that Rikki and Sasha weren't really worried. *They think I can lead them back to camp! And I have no idea where it is!*

Aaron knew better. But he had an idea. "We walked upstream, right? So if we go downstream, we should find our way back."

Rikki and Sasha looked at Kyle. "He's absolutely right," Kyle said. "Let's go."

The four kids started back down the creek, this time avoiding the cold water and walking along the bank. The dark mist made the trees look very strange, almost scary. Kyle had a sick feeling in his stomach, but it wasn't because he was afraid of the dark.

"Are we almost there, Kyle?" Sasha asked. "It seems like we've walked a long way."

Me and my bright ideas, Kyle thought. *Now the girls think I'm a super scout, and I'm just as lost as they are.* Then he thought of something else that made him feel even worse.

He stopped. "Wait a minute, everyone. We have a problem. How will we know when we get to the campsite? It's all the way up the hill. We could walk right past it."

Rikki flopped onto the ground. "That's right," she said. "We can't see the campsite from the creek. Come on, Kyle, do your thing and tell us how to get back."

Kyle hung his head. "I can't."

"What do you mean you can't?" Sasha asked. "Oh no, you don't have your compass."

Aaron glared at Kyle, but he didn't say anything. Kyle finally said it himself. "I tricked you this afternoon. I knew where we were all the time."

Rikki jumped up. "You mean we weren't really lost? Not at all?"

"You can see the big tree in the campground from almost anywhere," Kyle explained. "All we had to do was walk toward it."

Sasha stomped her foot. "And you let us wander around, worried sick?" She turned to Aaron. "I suppose you knew all about this little joke."

Kyle answered. "He knew about it, but it was my idea."

Rikki waved her hands. "Wait a minute. Then all we have to do is look for . . . oh no. We are really, totally lost now." She sank back to the ground.

"Yeah," Kyle admitted. "But I know what we should do."

Sasha glared at him. "I know what *you* should do. You should go soak your head in the creek."

"I have an idea," Aaron said. "Let's shout as loud as we can. If we are near the camp, Dad and Mom will hear us."

Everyone took a deep breath. "Help!" they shouted together. Then they listened. There was no answer.

"Help!" they shouted again, but there was still no answer.

"We must not be close to the camp," Rikki said with a sigh. "But are we too far upstream, or did we go past it?"

"I know what we should do," Kyle said again.

"What?" Rikki finally asked. "Hold our fingers in the air? Stand on our heads? What should we do?"

"Nothing," Kyle answered. "We should sit and wait right here by the creek. Our parents are probably already looking for us. They know we went to the creek, so that's where they'll look."

Rikki looked at Sasha. "Do you think he's right?"

"It's too dark to do anything else without a flashlight," Sasha said with a shiver. "Shhh! Did you hear that?"

They all listened and heard the leaves rustling nearby in the woods. "Whatever it is, it sounds big," Aaron said.

"Dad, is that you?" Kyle called. The rustling just got louder. They could barely see something moving. Suddenly, it came right at them. Sasha screamed . . . and the little raccoon making all the noise jumped and ran the other way.

Sasha put her head in her hands. "How could something so small make that much noise?"

After a few minutes, everyone was very quiet again. Then they heard a sound in the distance. "I thought I saw something," Aaron hissed. "Something that glows."

The sound got louder—and closer. Then—

"Rikki! Kyle! Where are you?"

"Dad! We're here!" Their dad's flashlight lit up a path to him, and everyone ran down it.

Later, Kyle sat and stared at the fire. With a cup of hot chocolate in his hands, he felt a lot better. "Sorry about tricking you guys," he said. "It was a mean thing to do."

"Well, you did the right thing tonight," his dad told them all. "You stayed by the creek, and when you weren't sure what to do, you stopped and waited. That's the best thing to do when you're lost."

"Even without a super scout, we made it back," Rikki said. Then she threw a twig at her brother. "If you ever do that again, I hope you get a frog in your pants!"

Austin's Butterfly Adventure

randma!" Austin called from in front of the bookshelf in the living room.

"What is it, Austin? I'm trying to fix lunch," she called back from the kitchen.

Austin stared at the encyclopedia set and called again. "Grandma, I need your help." After a minute, his grandmother appeared behind him, wiping her hands on a dish towel.

"What do you need, Austin? Why aren't you outside playing, like your sister?"

"Grandma, I have to finish my science report today, and I need help. Where do I look to find out about monarch butterflies? Under *B* or under *M*?"

Grandma reached for the *B* encyclopedia. "You bring this to the kitchen table and start reading while I finish the mashed potatoes."

From his seat at the table, Austin learned that butterflies eat nectar from flowers, like bees do. Then a small hand

Living by the golden rule

shook his arm. It was his little sister, Rita.

"Austin, come and help me in the backyard, OK?" she asked. Austin tried to ignore her. He kept reading.

"Austin, come and help me!"

"Grandma, Rita won't leave me alone so I can read this," Austin called. "Make her go away, please."

Grandma frowned at Austin but said, "Rita, don't bother Austin right now. Maybe he'll play with you later."

Rita started to explain. "But, Grandma, it'll only take a minute."

"Not now," her grandmother repeated. Rita stomped her foot and walked out. Austin went back to the encyclopedia.

"Austin," Grandma said when Rita was gone, "did you listen to the pastor in church this week? To what he said about the golden rule?"

Austin waved one hand at her. "The Bible says something about treating other people nice. But that's just church stuff. I'm trying to do my homework."

Grandma shook her head, but she didn't say anything.

Later, after lunch, Austin was writing about where monarch butterflies live. "Hey," he said to himself, "they even live around here." Just then, he heard a whisper at the window.

"Austin!" Rita whispered louder than most people talk. "Hurry, come out here and help me. It's right on the swing. We can catch it."

"No," Austin answered. "Go away." Then he picked up his stuff and went back to the bookshelf in the living room. After a few minutes, he was calling again.

"Grandma!"

He heard her voice. It sounded like she was a long way away. "What is it, Austin?"

"I need your help," he called back. While he waited, he searched through the pages and found a picture of a monarch butterfly. He heard his grandmother's footsteps in the hall and looked up as she came in the room. "I have to draw and color a butterfly for my report."

She looked tired. "Austin, I'm trying to get some things done too. I can't spend all afternoon helping you. You have a picture of a monarch there. Why do you need me?"

Austin frowned at the picture. "It's not a very good one. The butterfly's wings are up, and I wanted to draw one with the wings spread out."

Grandma helped him draw butterfly wings spread out on his page and made sure he had the right-color crayons. Then she left him at the table to finish his report. He had one wing colored when Rita came back.

"Austin," she said as the door slammed behind her, "come out here quick! It's right on the rosebush by my room. You have to help me." She grabbed his arm as she spoke.

"Hey, you almost made me mess up my report! Go away and leave me alone, OK?" His angry voice sent her right back out the door.

But Grandma walked in just as Rita left. "Austin, I heard the way you talked to your sister. All she wants is for you to take a few minutes and play with her."

Austin growled. "I want to finish this report. She just wants to show me some dumb thing she saw."

His grandmother didn't like that at all. "She just wants you to do the same thing you've been asking me to do all afternoon. She wants you to come and help her for a few minutes. Now go out there and do it!"

Austin dropped his crayon. He knew his grandmother was right, but he still didn't like it. He shuffled out the back door and stood on the step. "Rita, what . . ." he started to call, but something stopped him. From around the corner of the house came a butterfly with wings the same color as his drawing.

"It's a monarch!" he said out loud. Rita ran around the corner right behind it.

"Help me catch it," she called. "It's getting away." They ran under it as the butterfly floated up to the top of the swing set.

There it landed and waited as Austin slowly climbed the slide. Just as he reached the top, the butterfly floated up and then sailed away on a strong breeze. They watched until it disappeared down the street.

"If I could have caught it, I could have taken it to school tomorrow in a jar. My teacher would have liked my report even better with a real, live monarch butterfly as part of it. We could have turned it loose at recess," he told his grandmother as he and Rita had a glass of water in the kitchen.

"I've been trying to catch it all day," Rita added.

Austin looked at her. "Why didn't you tell me? Oh yeah, I guess you did try to tell me. And I wouldn't listen."

While he finished his report, Austin was still thinking about the butterfly that got away. "Grandma, if I had stopped to help Rita the way I wanted you to stop and help me all day, I'd have a butterfly."

Grandma nodded. "That's what the golden rule means. Treat others the way you want to be treated. You'll always end up happier, even if you don't get a butterfly."

"Is the Bible right about everything?"

Grandma smiled. "The Bible is God's way of telling you how to be happy."

Austin jumped up. "I told Rita I would hunt for butterflies with her as soon as I finished. Maybe we'll find another monarch!" He rushed to the back door, then stopped. "Thanks for everything, Grandma."

"You're welcome," she answered. Suddenly, she didn't feel so tired.

Dino-Monsters in the Dark

The shadow in the closet moved! This time, Bobby was sure of it. Even with just one eye peeking out from under the covers, he had seen it. And it looked like . . .

"Dad!"

"What is it, Bobby? You're supposed to be asleep by now." His voice sounded a long way away, even though Bobby knew he was just in the living room.

"Dad, I can't go to sleep."

This time Dad's voice came from the doorway. "Well, no wonder. You're probably too hot under all those covers. Crawl out and breathe some fresh air." He pulled the covers back and folded them toward the end of the bed.

"Uh, thanks, Dad." Bobby felt a lot better, but not because of the covers. The dark didn't seem scary at all with Dad there. "I guess I'm just not sleepy."

Dad sat on the bed beside him. "That's hard to believe after the busy day you had. Mom says you and Alan must

Fear of the dark

have run around this house a hundred times."

Bobby smiled. "Yeah. Sometimes, we shot ourselves with our squirt guns just to cool off." He yawned. "Dad, would you turn up the sound on the TV so I can hear it? It might help me go to sleep."

"OK," he said, "but just for a few minutes. Now close your eyes." Bobby pulled his covers back up, and with his eyes screwed tightly closed, he waited for the sound of the TV.

"The problems facing the trucking industry are examined in this story with Carmen Van Zant."

This ought to bore anyone to sleep, Bobby thought. And he kept his eyes closed until it worked.

The next day, he and Alan were scarfing down the spaghetti Bobby's mom had made for lunch. Even though Alan lived down the street, he ate lunch at Bobby's a lot in the summertime. "Bobby, are you going to summer camp? I'm going next month. It's great."

"It sounds boring," Bobby said between bites. "What do you do all day?"

"Oh, it's not boring." Alan waved his fork around. "We go horseback riding, canoeing, and swimming every day."

"Really? But I don't know how to ride a horse."

"No problem," Alan said. "They have classes in everything—horseback riding, swimming, archery, crafts, every-thing!"

"That does sound like fun, Bobby," his mom said.

"My favorite part is at campfire," Alan went on. "Everyone sings these great songs. Then we can roast marshmallows. I always take my flashlight so I can see the way back to the cabin."

Suddenly, it didn't seem like such a good idea. "No," Bobby said. "I wouldn't want to go."

"Why not?" Alan asked. "I know you'd like it."

Bobby just shook his head. "Come on. Let's go." He jumped up and swallowed the last of his juice. "I'll race you to the treehouse!"

That night, Bobby lay under his covers with his fists clenched. *I won't open my eyes. I won't be afraid,* he told him-self. Then he heard something over by the window. Before he could stop it, one eye popped open.

Right by the window was a shadow—and it looked like some kind of dinosaur-monster! "Dad!" Bobby called from under his covers. "Dad, I can't sleep."

His dad came in and almost pulled the covers back again. Instead, he sat down on the bed. "Bobby, what's wrong?"

Bobby's head popped out. "I just can't go to sleep."

"Are you sure that's it?" Dad asked, brushing back Bobby's hair with his fingers. "You sounded scared when you called me."

Bobby's face turned red in the dark. "Well, it sounds silly now, but . . . I guess I was a little scared. I heard something by the window, and then I saw a shadow that looked like some kind of dinosaur-monster."

"Over there?" Dad asked. He stood up and walked over by

the window. "Here?"

"Well, it doesn't look like it now," Bobby admitted. "But in the dark, shadows always look different—and scary."

Dad walked over and flipped the light switch. "See what's making that shadow?"

Right next to the window was Bobby's coat rack. And hanging on one hook was his baseball cap. "That's it?" Bobby sat up and laughed. "My baseball cap made it look like a dinosaur? Turn the light off again. Let me see if I can see it."

With the room dark again, Bobby strained his eyes. "I guess the bill of my cap looked like its jaws or something. It sure doesn't look scary now."

"Mom told me you weren't interested in summer camp. Is this why?" Dad asked as Bobby lay back down.

He nodded. "I don't want Alan or anyone to know that I'm still afraid of the dark. They'd say I was still a little kid."

"Lots of people are afraid of the dark. Even adults. And it's because they have a strong imagination, like you do." Dad snapped his fingers. "I've got an idea." He walked over to Bobby's closet and pulled something out. When he propped it on top of the closet door, he asked, "What do you see?"

"It's my kite," Bobby said. Then Dad turned off the light.

"Now what do you see?"

In the dark, Bobby wasn't sure. He squinted at the closet door. It looked like something with wings, but not a bird.

"How about an angel?" Dad asked.

"Yeah," Bobby decided, "it could be an angel. I like that."

Dad lay down beside Bobby on the bed. "If your imagination is going to see things, it might as well see things you like."

"Hey, that's right," Bobby agreed. "If the shadows can look

like monsters, they can look like angels. After all, I really do have angels watching me, don't I, Dad?"

"You sure do. That's what the Bible promises us. Now, after we practice this for a few weeks, do you think you might like to talk about going to summer camp?"

Bobby nodded. "Can we practice it outside too?"

"Yes. And remember, Alan said he always takes a flashlight to camp. We can get you the biggest flashlight in town."

"OK, Dad. Thanks." He wrapped his arms around his dad's neck.

"Now, you do have to go to sleep. Don't forget your angel."

Even after Dad left, Bobby kept smiling. He smiled at his cap by the window. He smiled at the angel on his closet door. He smiled himself to sleep.

"I HATE HIM/ I HATE HER"

RACHEL
I knew I didn't like him the first day of school. I told Emily, "Did you see that new kid? He's carrying a briefcase! Can you believe it?"

"Really?" Emily was amazed. "What is he, from another planet?"

Then we found out in homeroom. It wasn't another planet—just another continent. "Class," Mrs. O'Dell announced, "we have a new student this year. Jacob Costanza's family have recently moved back to America from Egypt. His parents were missionaries there.

Being a Christian; dealing with hatred

Now his father is the pastor at Southside Church."

I rolled my eyes at Emily. "Just what we needed," I whispered. "A preacher's kid. No wonder he's so weird."

In case you couldn't tell, I don't like preachers or their kids. In fact, I don't like Christians at all.

JACOB

I thought I would love coming back to America to go to school, but I don't. Everything is so different! I mean, I'm supposed to be an American, but I don't even know what American kids act like.

"Don't worry," Mom said. "You'll fit in fine." Then she sent me off to the first day of school with a briefcase. I thought I would die of embarrassment!

"Mom," I reported that afternoon, "no one in America takes a briefcase to school. They all carry backpacks, or nothing."

"Backpacks?" she asked. "Like they were camping and hiking? How very odd."

"No, Mom, just me. I'm the only one who's odd."

After that first day, it wasn't so bad. In fact, most of the kids are pretty friendly—except for Rachel. She really hates me. And I don't know why. Maybe I should try to be more friendly to her.

RACHEL

I'm going to die! I have never been so embarrassed in my whole life! I was eating lunch in the cafeteria at my usual table, with Emily, when Jacob just walked up and sat down like he belonged there.

"Hi," he said with a toothy smile.

"Hi, Jacob," Emily said.

I said, "Jacob—that's a name from the Bible, right? I guess that's a good name for a preacher's kid." He just took out his lunch. "What's that?" I asked politely.

"It's a kind of Egyptian food," he said. "It's called falafel [fuh-law-ful]."

I wrinkled my nose. "I think I'd call it 'smell-awful.' " Everyone laughed. Even Jacob.

Then smart-mouth Andy said it. "Hey, wasn't the Jacob in the Bible married to Rachel?"

I thought I was going to die. Everyone laughed. Andy couldn't shut up. "Rachel and Jacob. Jacob and Rachel. I guess they're supposed to be together."

Before they even finished laughing, I had decided two things. The first one was about my name. "Emily," I said later, "from now on, my name is Rach. Don't ever call me Rachel again."

The second thing was this: I'm going to make Jacob wish he had never come back to America.

JACOB

All I did was try to be friendly. I didn't point out that her name was from the Bible too. I even laughed at her stupid joke about my food. But now Rachel really hates me.

I'm getting along fine with the others. Andy picked me to be on his football team at recess. Then he said, "Jacob, grab the football. Let's get to the field before anyone else and practice passing."

So I grabbed the football and ran after him. But as soon as I kicked it, he looked at me like I was crazy. Rachel was right behind us. "Hey, Bible boy," she called, "don't you even know the difference between a football and a soccer ball?"

Then I remembered. "They call soccer 'football' in Egypt. I forgot you meant American football."

Rachel wouldn't let it go. "Well, if you like Egyptian things so much, why don't you go back there. No one wants you here anyway."

I knew she was trying to make me mad. It worked. I threw the football down and stomped away.

I hate Rachel.

RACHEL

"Rach, why do you hate Jacob so much?" Emily asked. "You always call him 'Bible boy' and go out of your way to be mean to him."

I shrugged. "I just do. All those goody-goody Christians make me sick. My mom says no one believes those stories anyway."

"Didn't you used to go to church? Before your parents split up?"

"That's why I hate church," I explained. "My dad always went and acted so perfect. And at home, he would read the Bible to us. Then one day he just left, like he didn't even care about us. If that's what Christians are like, I hate them."

I just know that Jacob is as fake as my father was. And I'm going to make him mad enough to prove that to everyone.

JACOB

"Dad," I asked one night, "is it OK to hate someone who hates you first?"

Dad frowned. "Jacob, the Bible is pretty clear about not hating anyone."

"What if I just don't like someone? What if I don't like them so much I wish they would walk in front of a moving bus?"

"You know," Dad said, "Jesus had to deal with people who hated Him. Do you know what He did and what He taught His followers to do?"

"What?"

"He treated them with kindness. Return good for evil, He told them. That's what being a Christian is all about. Is this person who hates you a Christian?"

"Rachel? She hates Christians. At least, that's what she tells everyone."

Dad thought for a moment. "Then I guess you can show her what a Christian is really like. I'll be praying for you, Jacob."

I think I'd better be praying too.

RACHEL

That Jacob makes me so mad! I poured milk on his lunch. I "accidentally" knocked his books off his desk. I even threw his homework in the trash. But he just smiles and says nothing.

JACOB

God, if Rachel does one more thing to me, I'm going to strangle her! Unless You help me. Please help me return kindness for evil. Amen.

RACHEL

I can't believe it! Mrs. O'Dell can't make me do it, can she?

JACOB

Just when I thought it couldn't get worse, it did!

SOUVENIRS

RACHEL

"You'll be giving reports on countries of the world," Mrs. O'Dell said. As if that wasn't bad enough, she added more. "And you'll be working in groups of three."

I knew she'd let Emily and me work together—we always do. But our other partner was the big shock. Mrs. O'Dell announced it loud and clear. "Our first group will be Emily, Rachel, and Jacob."

I argued with her. I even begged. "Mrs. O'Dell, we can't work with him—he's a boy." I couldn't really tell her that I hate him. "Please give us another girl."

"Nonsense, Rachel," was her only answer. "You'll do fine."

At lunch, Emily was happy. "This will be fun. Jacob's probably the one person in our class who's been to some other countries."

"He'll probably want to do our report on some Bible land,"

Being a Christian; faith in the Bible

I grumbled.

That afternoon, Mrs. O'Dell gave everyone time to begin working with their partners. Emily and I pulled our desks up by Jacob's. "Look, Bible boy," I said right away, "we're not doing this report on Israel or some other Bible land. Everyone knows those stories aren't real anyway."

I saw his mouth open and close. He almost got mad and shouted at me. Maybe this will work out after all. . . .

JACOB

I wish Rachel would stop calling me "Bible boy."

It's not my fault Mrs. O'Dell put us together. And I didn't say anything about any Bible lands. But when she started saying the Bible stories are made-up, I almost let her have a piece of my mind.

"Mom, what am I going to do?" I asked after school. "Rachel hates me, but I have to do this report with her and Emily."

"Why don't you invite them to come over here after school and work on the report? We have encyclopedias and everything. I could make some cookies."

I guess it's a good idea. Unless Rachel tries to burn down my house or something.

RACHEL

I guess it makes sense. But I don't like it. Emily wanted to do it as soon as Mrs. O'Dell explained the assignment.

"Class, your reports need to tell where the country is, how many people live there, and something about the way they live. I want pictures that show what the people usually wear, what their houses look like, and what kind of land their country is."

"Rach, we've got to do our report on Egypt," Emily said. "No one else can say they lived in a different country. With Jacob, we'll get the best grade in the class."

"I guess you're right," I agreed. "But I don't have to like it—or him."

When we got together for social studies, I let Emily do the talking. "Jacob, why don't we do our report on Egypt? You could probably tell the class a lot of stuff we wouldn't find in an encyclopedia."

You'll never guess what he did. He invited us to his house to work on the report. Both of us!

JACOB

Well, I wouldn't have believed it, but Rachel and Emily came to my house. Mom was great. "More cookies, girls?" she asked. She makes the best oatmeal-raisin cookies.

"Mrs. Costanza," Emily said between bites, "we want to do our report on Egypt, since Jacob lived there."

"Why, that's a fine idea," she agreed. "Jacob, have you shown them your souvenirs?"

So I took them to my room to show off my collection of keepsakes and stuff. Emily started looking before I could even show her.

"What is this?" she asked, holding up an Egyptian flute. I told her. "What's this?" An Egyptian hat, I explained. While I was showing her the Egyptian sculptures and basket, I kept turning my head to keep an eye on Rachel. She was looking at my other stuff, and I didn't want her breaking it or anything.

"Are these Egyptian coins?" Emily asked. Before I could answer, Rachel interrupted.

"Have you really been to all these places?"

RACHEL

I stared at a silver mouse and a picture of Jacob and his mother with Donald Duck. Disneyland, I'm sure. Then there was the little statue of the Washington Monument. And a picture of him and his dad in front of the Lincoln Memorial. Washington, D.C.

"Are you guys rich?" I asked.

"No. Missionaries just travel a lot."

There were things from Paris and London. But a funny-looking picture caught my eye. "What's this?"

"You're not going to like it," he said. "It's a picture of me and my dad in a cave under Jerusalem. That tunnel leads up to the city. But they wouldn't let us climb it."

I just stared.

"It's from the story in the Bible—where David's men capture the city by climbing up the tunnel."

I knew that story. "It's real? That place is really there? Still?"

"Cool," Emily said, walking over to look. "What are these rocks?"

You won't believe what he said.

JACOB

"You remember the story of David and Goliath?" I asked. "And how David picked up the stones from the stream for his sling?" They nodded. "I went there. To the same valley. These stones are from that same stream."

I thought Rachel was going to faint. Instead, she sat down on my bed. "I can't believe it," was all she said.

We didn't get much done on our report. Rachel was ready to leave. I don't know if that's good or not.

I hope I did the right thing, telling her that Bible stuff.

RACHEL

"You don't think Jacob was just making up that stuff about the Bible stories, do you?" I asked Emily.

"Rach, do you think he was making up the stuff about Disneyland? Or Washington, D.C.?"

She's right. Of course, he's not. But that means the stories in the Bible are real. And that Jacob is a real Christian. Look at all the mean things I've done to him! And he's always been nice.

Maybe Christians aren't as bad as I thought. I'd better talk to Mom about this.

JACOB

Wow! Something sure changed. Rachel was actually nice to me today. I wonder what that means?

RACHEL

I surprised Emily at lunchtime. I said, "Let's sit with Jacob."

She looked at me. "Rach, what's going on? Are you feeling OK?"

"I'm feeling fine," I told her. "And, Emily—call me Rachel."

"It Might Happen!"

17

OK, so maybe I was worrying too much. But you know how it is—when you hear about things you don't want to happen to you, you worry. At least I do.

"Mom, should I wear my raincoat?" I was looking at the sky. Most of it was blue, but there was one cloud. "It could rain."

"Mitch, it's not going to rain. The newspaper said that it's supposed to be sunny today. Now go, before you miss the bus."

"But, Mom, if it rains and I get wet walking home from the bus stop, I might get sick. Then I would miss a quiz in math class. I'd get a bad grade."

I knew it could happen—Matthew was sick last week. Right now, he has an "F".

Dealing with worry

"Mitch! Go before you miss the bus!"

I keep a list of things that might happen, things to worry about. I don't want these kinds of things happening to me.

What Might Happen	What to Do
Fire at home	Practice jumping from window
Lightning strikes	Keep low
Math quiz	Study every night
Rain	Wear raincoat every day

On the way to school, we passed an accident. That made me think. "Mr. Montori," I called out, "what would happen if we crashed and you were knocked out? Who would take over?"

He glanced at me in the big mirror and smiled. "You would, Mitch," he said.

You know what I started doing then. Worrying.

That night, I tried to ask my dad about it. "Just a minute," he said. He was glued to the TV news. "I want to hear this." The reporter was standing in front of a school.

"School officials are not calling it a measles epidemic yet," the reporter said, "but more than twenty kids from this school are home scratching at red spots."

Suddenly, I had an itch on my neck. And maybe one on my back.

"At least that's not your school," Dad said. "Mitch! What are you doing?"

"Itching."

"Well, stop. You had a measles vaccination years ago. What did you want to ask me?"

"Dad, I need to learn how to drive." He looked at me like I

was speaking a foreign language. "I guess we could start with driving a car and then . . ."

"You? Drive? Why?"

"In case the school bus crashes and someone has to take over. If I know how to drive, I can do it."

For some reason, Dad put his head in his hands. "No wonder my hair is falling out," he muttered.

"Dad, it might happen."

"Mitch, you can't drive. Even if you knew how, you're not big enough to reach the pedals—especially on a bus. And even if you could, you're not old enough."

"But what if we crash?"

"You'll wait for the police. If you can help, Mitch, it will be by going to find an adult." Dad turned back to the TV. "You can't worry about everything, Mitch. Look at me—I don't worry."

I wasn't sure I believed him. "You mean you're not worried that your hair is falling out?"

"No, Mitch," Dad said with a chuckle, "I'm not. It's just something that happens to the men in my family. Now, let me

"It Might Happen!"

finish watching the news, will you?"

That gave me something else to think about. And to add to my list.

What Might Happen	What To Do
Fire at home	Practice jumping from window
Lightning strikes	Stay low
Math quiz	Study every night
Rain	Wear raincoat at all times
Bus crash	~~Learn to drive~~ Go get help
~~Measles~~	~~Never mind~~
Go bald	Find a way to grow hair

OK, maybe I was a little too worried about going bald. But what would you do if you found out that your hair could fall out at any time?

I finally got an idea in P.E. "Mom," I called when I came in the door, "I have a note for you from Coach Gonzales."

"You're not in trouble, are you?" She took the note and read it. "You want to start lifting weights? Why?"

I flexed my arm muscle. "Coach told me that lifting weights will help my arm muscles grow. I'm hoping there are weights to make all the parts of my body grow."

She just stared for a second, then shook her head. "Coach says that we should have your back checked by a doctor first. He says you walk hunched over a lot."

"Just trying to stay low," I explained. She looked blank. "In case of lightning," I added. She got a pained look on her face.

It was Dad who saw me in front of the mirror later that week. "Mitch, what are you doing—trying to see if your eyebrows will come loose?"

"I'm exercising," I explained. It was an exercise workout I had figured out for myself. I wiggled my eyebrows up and down ten times. Then I opened my eyes as wide as they would go ten times. Next, I tried to wiggle my ears. I still hadn't figured that part out very well.

"Are they making you lift weights with your eyebrows now?" Dad asked.

"No, Dad, don't be ridiculous. These are my hair exercises. So my hair will stay strong and grow instead of falling out."

He got a pained look like Mom's. "Mitch, you seem to be worried about a lot of things lately. What's wrong?"

I tried to explain. "I just don't want bad things to happen to me. So I'm planning ahead. Isn't that what I should do?"

"Mitch, when I was about your age, I asked my dad if he was worried about going bald. Of course, he was a lot balder then than I am now. He said, 'If worrying would help, I'd stay home three days a week and grow hair.' "

I thought about it. "He meant that worrying wouldn't help."

"That's right. It just keeps you from enjoying today," Dad finished. "If there's something you *can do*—"

"Like wear your raincoat," I interrupted. "Or study for your math quizzes."

"Right," Dad agreed, "then you should do it. Otherwise—"

"Don't worry about it," I finished. "I get it."

So I decided not to worry so much. And I already feel better. Those hair exercises were giving me a headache.

Crossing the Boundary

Crystal tipped her sunglasses down and squinted over the top. "Who? Where?"

"Over there." Erin pointed across the sandy beach. "See, those two at the edge of the water."

Crystal looked. "Oh, gross. They are kissing! Right here in front of everyone." Erin made gagging noises, but both girls watched until the couple walked away.

"I'm not ever letting someone kiss me like that," Crystal declared as she lay back down on her towel.

"I don't know," Erin answered. "My sister Melody says it's nice. She kisses her boyfriend all the time."

Crystal slapped some sand onto her friend's leg. "I'm hot. Race you to the rope!" Dropping her sunglasses onto her towel, Crystal dashed across the sand to the cool water. As she slashed through the shallow waves, she could hear Erin right behind her. Finally, it was deep enough to dive in and swim.

Learning about sex; AIDS

Crossing the Boundary

Between strokes, Crystal could see the yellow rope rise and fall with the waves. A few more kicks brought her close enough to stand up. "I won!" she called as Erin stood up beside her.

Erin tipped her head back into the water and came up with her hair plastered back. "I used to think this place was magic," she said. "You know, because the water was too deep for me to walk in, but I could see people out here walking around."

Crystal laughed. "Yeah, me too. Until I learned about the sandbars. It is weird that the water is shallow, then deep, then shallow again." She looked out into the bay. "I always wondered if it kept doing this all the way across the ocean. You know, like maybe there was a place out in the middle of the ocean where you could just stand up."

"Did you ever go past the rope?" Erin asked. "And tell the truth."

Crystal was horrified. "No! Not after my dad told me about being here when a man swam out there. The undertow current pulled him farther and farther out, and he couldn't swim back. He drowned." She shivered. "Did you?"

Erin nodded. "Once, last summer. I thought maybe people were just telling me about the undertow and sharp rocks to scare me. I just wanted to see how far I could walk before it got deep again. So I waited until Mom wasn't looking and hopped over the rope."

Crystal's eyes got big. "Really? What happened?"

"Well, I didn't drown!" Erin laughed just for a second. "But everyone thought I was going to. I took a few steps away from the rope, and the bottom disappeared. It got really deep!"

"What did you do?"

"I started swimming back in. But by then, the lifeguard was blowing his whistle and racing out toward me. Mom was screaming. She came across and grabbed me like I was about to die."

Crystal shook her head. "So there really isn't an undertow that pulls you out?"

Erin shrugged. "The lifeguard said it wasn't very strong that day. And I didn't go very far. But he said some days I would have been caught for sure." She grinned sheepishly. "My dad had to pay a fine. And I wasn't allowed to swim here for a whole month."

Crystal looked into the deep blue water beyond the rope and shivered again. "Come on. Let's go back in."

After a few minutes warming in the sun, both girls were ready to go. "Come on. Let's go to my house first," Erin said. "I'll change, and then we'll go to your house."

Since they lived only a block apart, Erin and Crystal spent

Crossing the Boundary

a lot of time at each other's homes. They came in through Erin's backyard. As Erin pulled the screen door open, they both heard it. Someone inside the house was crying. Crying hard and loud. Erin froze.

"What is it?" Crystal whispered. "What's wrong?"

"I don't know," Erin hissed. "But it must be something really bad."

Then they heard Erin's dad's voice. He was shouting. "Melody, do you understand what this means? High school, the basketball team, your senior trip—all that is over."

Erin's mom spoke. Her voice sounded shaky. "Stop shouting, Steve. I think she understands. Melody, are you sure? Have you been to a doctor?"

That brought more crying sounds from Erin's sister.

Crystal shook her friend. "Erin, maybe I should go."

Erin turned to grab Crystal's arm. "Please don't." But when she turned, the door slipped out of her hand and slammed shut. They both heard footsteps. Then Erin's mom appeared.

"Erin, say goodbye to your friend, and come in, please."

Just from looking at her, Crystal knew Erin's mother had been crying too. "I'll call you later, Erin," she said. Then she ran all the way home.

When Crystal got to her house, she was panting and sweating. Her mom was chopping lettuce at the sink. "What's wrong?" she asked as soon as she saw Crystal's face.

Crystal got a glass of water and plopped down on a stool before she answered. "I don't know, really. Something bad."

Mom chopped at the lettuce again. "Should I guess? Does it have something to do with Erin?"

"Not really Erin." Crystal sipped at her water.

"Something's wrong with her sister, Melody. She's sick or something. She'll probably go to the hospital. Or die."

Mom looked up. "That bad, huh? What makes you think so?"

"Well, the way she was crying, it has to be something bad. And her mom was crying too. And her dad was all upset." Crystal stared down into her glass. "I wouldn't be surprised if she was dead already," she said darkly.

"Maybe I should call and see if there's anything I can do," Mom said, setting down her knife.

"No, not now," Crystal said. "I told Erin I'd call her later." She waited until after supper. Then she dialed Erin's number.

Erin's dad answered. "Hello!" he almost shouted. "Who is it?"

"It's C-crystal," Crystal stammered. "Can I talk to Erin?"

"Oh." His voice softened. "Sure. Erin, it's for you."

Crystal waited. Then she heard Erin's voice. "Hi. Just a second." After a few more thumps, Erin spoke again. "Now we can talk."

"You sound funny," Crystal said, "like you're in a tunnel or something."

"That's because I'm in the closet. It's the only way we can talk. Everyone's still pretty upset around here."

"Is she really sick?" Crystal asked. "Is she going to die?"

Erin giggled nervously. "No, she's not going to die. She's going to have a baby."

Crystal almost dropped the phone.

Safe and Happy

19

"She's pregnant?" Crystal could hardly believe her ears. "But she's not even married."

"I guess you don't have to be married," Erin said. "You just have to have sex with your boyfriend. At least, that's what Melody did."

"No wonder your mom and dad were so upset. I guess they're glad she's not dying or something, though."

"I guess. But they don't sound too glad right now. Wait a second." Even over the phone, Crystal could hear the sound of someone knocking on the closet door. "OK," Erin said. Then, "Crystal, I have to go. Mom wants to use the phone. I'll talk to you later."

When Crystal hung up, she went and collapsed onto the couch beside her

Learning about sex; AIDS

mother. "Mom, guess what?" she said over the sound of the television. Her mother's eyes were glued to the picture.

"Mom!"

Her mother turned and looked at her. "What is it, Crystal? I'm trying to watch this show."

"Mom, Erin's sister is pregnant. She's going to have a baby. You told me that people had to get married before they could have a baby."

Her mom stared at her for a second, then clicked the TV off. "Crystal, I told you that people get married, then have a baby. That's what they should do. That's the way God designed it to work."

"But . . ."

"But Melody and her boyfriend made a choice to not stop at just kissing and hugging. They had sex together."

Crystal made a gagging sound. "Please, Mom. Don't gross me out." Her mom had explained about sex and reproducing last year. She didn't really want to hear about it again. "Why would they do that?"

Mom sighed. "Because when your body is grown up, it feels nice, and it makes you feel as if someone loves you. You may not be interested in boys now, Crystal, but you will be one of these days."

From the look on her face, Crystal made it clear that she found that hard to believe. Mom went on.

"And you'll have to make choices about your body and your future. Too many people think of sex as some kind of game. They do it just for fun. I hope you remember that God's plan is to save sex until after you're married. And His plan is there to protect your happiness."

Crystal was quiet for a moment. Then she asked, "Mom,

will Melody ever be happy again?"

Mom put her arms around Crystal. "Sure, she will be. But now she has to make a lot of grown-up decisions, and she isn't really grown up. It'll be hard for a while, but her family loves her, and she'll be all right."

"I'm going to wait until I'm married, Mom," Crystal said, snuggling in tighter. "If I decide to get married."

"I hope you do," Mom answered with a smile. "As bad as it seems, getting pregnant isn't the worst thing that could have happened to Melody. There are diseases you can get by having sex with a person who is infected. Diseases that can kill you."

"You mean like AIDS?" Crystal asked. She had heard about that at school. She knew that many people had died with it.

Several days went by before Crystal and Erin got to go back to the beach together. The first thing they did was swim out to the rope and sit in the shallow water, bobbing up and down with the waves. "Have your parents stopped shouting and crying?" Crystal asked.

"Mostly," Erin said. "Mom still looks sad all the time, and Daddy mumbles under his breath a lot. But Melody smiles more now."

"What is she going to do?"

Erin shrugged. "She doesn't know. She still doesn't know if she'll even get to finish school."

"Oh yeah." Crystal frowned. "She'll miss all her class parties and pro-grams."

"She won't get to play basketball much longer. And she is the best player on the team."

Crystal watched a wave coming in and felt herself rise up off the sand as it went past. "Did you ask Melody why she did it?"

"Yeah. Mostly, she said I wouldn't understand. But she said it was nice, like kissing. I wonder if it really is."

"My mom said it is nice too," Crystal said. "But she says it's a lot nicer if you wait until you're married."

"Why?"

"Because that's the way God made us." Crystal reached out and grabbed the yellow rope. She pushed it down and tried to stand on it.

A megaphone voice from the beach said, "Stay off the boundary rope, please. Stay inside the rope at all times."

Crystal jumped off and waved at the lifeguard. Then she settled back down by Erin. "Mom said God made sex with boundaries to keep us safe and happy. Kind of like the rope, I guess."

"You mean because His plan keeps us from getting involved with sex before we're married?" Erin asked. "I knew sex sounded gross, but I didn't know it was dangerous."

Crystal nodded. "You didn't know the undertow was dangerous, either. But the rope was here to protect you from dangers you couldn't see and didn't really understand."

"I went across it, and I didn't die," Erin reminded her.

Another wave lifted them both up. "But you had to pay for it. Melody won't die either," Crystal said, "but she'll have to pay for crossing the boundary. For a long time."

Erin stared across the water. "Yeah. I think you're right. I'm staying on this side." Then she shivered. "I'm freezing. Come on. I'll race you back."

30,000 FEET UP AND ARGUING

Yes, it is."

Scott ground his teeth together. "No, it's not, Nicholas."

"Yes, it is."

"No, it's—"

"Scott," Dad interrupted. "What is the argument about this time?"

Scott turned away from the airport window and looked at his father. "Dad, Nicholas keeps saying that the jet we're getting on is the biggest one in the world."

"And?"

"And it isn't! Everyone knows that there are lots of planes that are bigger. Nicholas just won't admit it."

Dad sighed. "Let it go, Scott. It doesn't really matter."

It matters to me, Scott thought as he turned back to stare at the planes coming and going. *I'm right, and he's wrong.*

The woman behind the ticket counter spoke into her

Arguing and quarreling

microphone. "We are now boarding passengers in rows ten through twenty-eight."

Scott looked over at his dad. "I guess that's us," he said.

"It's about time," Dad agreed. "I thought we were going to have to wait forever for your first plane ride. Now, where's your brother—Nicholas, let's go."

Scott followed them down the jetway. He didn't want to admit it, but he felt a little nervous. Nicholas didn't seem to be. "I want to sit by the window," Nicholas announced. For about the thousandth time.

"We've already had this discussion," Dad said quickly. "We agreed that you could sit by the window for the first half of the trip, then Scott will on the last half."

Scott looked at his ticket. *I'm supposed to sit by the window the whole way,* he said to himself. But he didn't say it out loud.

Before long, they were seated and buckled in. A voice spoke from the speaker over their heads. "Welcome aboard, this is your captain speaking. We'll be taxiing out to the runway for the next few minutes. Please pay attention while the flight attendants demonstrate the safety features of our airplane."

Scott watched the man in the aisle show how to buckle the seat belts and what to do if oxygen masks came down. "In case of a water landing, your seat cushion becomes a floatation device," he said.

"What does that mean?" Scott asked his dad. "Do our seats float?"

"No, just the cushion you're sitting on," Dad explained. "It comes loose and like a life jacket will help you float if we land in water."

"If we crash in the water, I'm not going to float," Nicholas declared. "I'm swimming to shore."

"What if we're five miles from land?" Scott asked.

"I'd still swim," Nicholas decided.

"You can't swim that far," Scott said. "You're not strong enough."

"Yes, I can," Nicholas answered. "I am *too* strong enough."

"No, you're not."

"Yes, I am."

"Boys!" Dad held up both hands. "Let's agree that no one will speak until the plane is in the air. OK? Just nod to answer."

Scott nodded and sat back. The captain's voice came on again. "Prepare for takeoff," he said. Before Scott was ready, the plane started going faster. The shaking and vibrating got worse. The noise of the jet engines got much louder. Scott tightened his grip on the armrests. He glanced over at his brother.

Nicholas was trying to lean forward so he could see out the window. He wasn't holding on at all.

Just when Scott was sure the plane was going to crash or fall apart, the front tipped up, and they were off the ground. It was a lot smoother, but it felt even stranger.

"Oh, wow. Look at that!" Nicholas called. Scott closed his eyes until he got used to the feeling of being in the air.

"Feeling better?" his dad asked a few minutes later.

"Uh, yeah," Scott said. "It just felt a little weird, that's all."

"I know," Dad agreed. "It makes me feel the same way. But you get used to it." He glanced at Nicholas. "Look at him—just like his mother. Flying never bothers her at all."

Scott frowned. "Nicholas and I are not much alike, are we?"

"No, you're not. I think that's why you argue so much. But, Scott, I don't think you're ever going to argue him into changing his mind. At least, I have never argued your mother into changing hers."

Scott thought about that. *Even if he's wrong? He won't change his mind?*

When they got farther from the ground, Nicholas got bored with the window. "Can I get up and walk around?" he asked.

"Not until the captain turns off the seat belt sign," Dad answered, pointing to the little symbol of a seat belt up by the speaker above them.

Before long, the captain did just that. "We should have a smooth flight, so feel free to move around in the cabin," he announced.

Nicholas unsnapped his belt. "I need to go to the bathroom," he announced.

"I'll go with you," Dad said. When they were gone, Scott popped his seat belt off and slid over to the window. He stared out at the puffy clouds and the ground far below. *How could anyone get bored looking at this?* he wondered.

For some reason, in spite of the loud noise of the engines, he could hear the conversation of the two men in front of him. They were arguing. "No way," one said. "The Panthers are the best team. They've won the most games!"

"I say the Red Dogs are better," the other one replied. "By the end of the season, everyone will know I'm right."

Yes! Scott agreed silently. *You're absolutely right, and he's wrong.*

30,000 Feet Up and Arguing

"Well, I guess we'll just have to agree to disagree," the first man decided. "You can think what you want, and I'll think what I want. I know I'm right anyway!"

They laughed and started talking about something else, but Scott kept thinking about it. *Agree to disagree,* he thought. *Even if you know you're right?*

Nicholas and Dad were back before long, and it didn't take long to find another argument. Nicholas was sitting by the window. "I saw a balloon," he announced. "One of those red kind, like I had at my birthday party."

"No, you didn't," Scott said automatically. "A birthday balloon couldn't get this high."

"Yes, it could," Nicholas said.

"No, it—" Scott stopped. He looked at his dad's growing frown. "Well, you think what you want, and I'll think what I want. We'll just agree to disagree."

Nicholas was confused. "Yes, I—uh—OK, I guess."

Dad was confused too. "Hey, I like the sound of that."

"Well," Scott said with a little smile, "I just think differently than Nicholas does. I know I'm right," he added. "But I guess it's OK if he thinks he is too."

Gramma Rose's Benster

Mom, this place is creepy." Brian wrinkled his nose as he followed his mother into the nursing home. "And it smells old."

"I don't know if the place is old," his mother answered, "but the people are. Come on, Gramma Rose's room is this way." Brian's mother usually visited Gramma Rose, Brian's great-grandmother on dad's side of the family, at least once a week.

Brian followed his mother, weaving past the silver wheelchairs with their silver-haired drivers. When they stopped to let a nurse go by, a cold hand latched onto his arm.

"Come here, sonny," an old woman croaked. "I need you."

Accepting older people; grandparents

"Mom," Brian hissed. The woman wouldn't let go. His mother turned and placed her hand on the woman's fingers.

"Good afternoon, ma'am," she said as she lifted the fingers from Brian's arm. "How are you today?"

The woman brought her hand back to her lap and seemed to fall asleep. Brian stepped away. "See, I told you. Creepy. What did she want?" he hissed.

"She's just very old and confused, Brian. Don't worry about it." Pushing open a blue door with the number 119 on it, Mom called, "Gramma Rose, we're here."

Once again, Brian was amazed to see the big smile on Gramma Rose's face. Somehow, he expected an old person to look grumpy or sad. But Gramma Rose was always happy, always smiling.

"Well, hello," Gramma Rose said from the chair she sat in. "And who are you?"

"It's Elaine, Gramma Rose," Mom said in a loud voice. "Elaine and Brian."

Brian saw the confused look on her face turn into a smile followed by a hug. "Elaine, how nice to see you. Where's Morty? Is he here?" She peered past Mom to where Brian stood.

"No, just me and Brian."

Gramma Rose nodded and smiled. "That Morty—he's such a cutup. I told his mother he'd always be a cutup."

That was one thing Brian could agree with. His Uncle Morty was always joking and teasing and . . . well, cutting up. Suddenly, Gramma Rose walked over to him.

"And who are you?" she asked. Smiling.

"Brian," he answered, leaning toward her. "I'm Brian." Then he waited and watched her face. *Will she do it this time?*

"Benster! Oh, it's good to see you, Benster."

It was the same as always. Brian returned her hug carefully. "I'm afraid she'll break," he always told his mom.

"Gramma Rose," Mom said, "it's almost your birthday. We're planning a party for next week."

"A party? For me?" Brian saw the excitement as her eyebrows went up and lifted her wrinkles. "Where's the cake?"

"Not today, Gramma Rose. Next week. Everyone's coming to my house for your birthday. You're coming too, aren't you?"

"Oh yes!" Gramma Rose clapped her hands. "I'll be there. You're coming, aren't you, Benster?" She grabbed his hands and did a kind of shuffling jig.

"I'll be there," Brian promised.

"Mom," Brian asked on the way home, "does Gramma Rose even know who I am? She always calls me Benster."

Mom shook her head. "Maybe that's just her nickname for you. I really don't know. She is confused about a lot of things. But she's sure happy to see you every time."

"Yeah." Brian had to agree. "Mom, why do you visit her so much? She's not your grandmother."

"She's someone I love, Brian. She was your father's grandmother. Your father had great memories of playing at her house as he grew up. He loved her dearly, and I learned to love her too."

Brian was quiet for a second. Then he asked a question that had been bothering him for a long time. "How come she never asks about Dad? She always recognizes you and asks about Uncle Morty. Didn't she like Dad?"

Mom parked in the driveway before she answered. "Brian, Gramma Rose loved your dad very much. When he was killed, she cried right along with your grandmother. And me,"

Gramma Rose's Benster

she added softly. "I don't know why she never asks. Maybe she has forgotten him. Maybe that was easier than remembering he's gone."

The next week, Brian answered the doorbell. His grandmother stood on the porch. "Grandma! You made it!"

"Brian, I think you grow taller every time I turn my back. And you look more like your father." After a hug, Brian grabbed her bags and followed her into the living room. "Elaine," she called to Brian's mother, "is there anything I can do to help you with the party?"

Brian's mother came out drying her hands on a dish towel. "Mother, sit down and rest for a moment. Everything's ready. It's so good to see you."

Brian watched more than listened as the two most important people in his life caught up on each other's news. *I wonder if Dad was like his mother, my grandma,* he thought. *I wish I could remember him better. I wonder if I'm like my mom.*

Before long, Gramma Rose and the other guests had

arrived, and the party began. As always, Gramma Rose was smiling. "Where's Morty?" she asked.

"He'll be here later," Brian's mother explained. "Come on now. Brian's serving the cake."

Gramma Rose looked at Brian. "And who are you?" she asked.

"I'm Brian," he answered, setting her slice on her plate.

Her confusion turned into a smile. "Benster! Oh, it's good to see you, Benster." Brian just smiled and kept slicing. Later, when Gramma Rose was napping in the easy chair, he flopped down on the couch beside his mom and grandmother.

"Grandma, do you think Gramma Rose has forgotten Dad? She never asks about him."

Grandma stroked his hair. "I don't know, Brian. She forgets more every year."

"I wish she could remember me," Brian grumbled. "She never knows who I am, and she can't remember my name. She always calls me Benster."

Grandma sat up straight. "What? What does she call you?"

"Benster. Do you know why?"

Grandma's eyes filled with tears. "Oh, Brian. That's what she called your father when he was a boy. Morty was always a 'cutup.' But she called your father 'Ben, her little monster,' until it turned into Benster."

Brian's mom was crying too. "That's why she never asks about your dad. She thinks you're him. The way she remembers him as a child."

"Really?" Brian turned to stare at his great-grandmother. "No wonder it makes her so happy to see me. I think I like that."

And he smiled.

GOOD-FOR-NOTHING SPECIAL

The rain pounded on Carly's poncho all the way down the street. *Is it never going to stop?* she wondered. For three straight days, rain had fallen. And Carly, along with the rest of the town, was tired of it.

Ding-ding! The bell on the diner door greeted Carly the way it greeted everyone. So did the woman in the blue apron behind the counter.

"Welcome to the Dark River Diner. Someone will be with you in a moment. Oh, Carly, it's you. Come help your poor, tired aunt for a minute."

"Sure, Aunt Frannie. Let me hang up this wet thing and set my books down." Carly dropped her books behind the counter and moved over to the cash register. "I told Mom that I would stop and help if you needed me." Aunt Frannie collapsed onto a nearby chair.

"Hi," Carly said as a customer walked up a moment later.

"Think this rain will ever stop?" he asked as he handed

Self-esteem; dealing with a new baby

Carly the bill for his meal.

Aunt Frannie answered. "Sheriff Hagerty was in here this morning. He says another couple of days like this, and Dark River will be in all our living rooms."

Carly punched the cash register buttons. "That'll be six ninety-eight. Thanks for stopping by."

"Carly, why don't you just take over and I'll retire," Aunt Frannie said. "I'm too old for this."

"No, you're not." Carly laughed. "You're just tired because Mom's not here to help you."

Aunt Frannie nodded. "Imagine her wanting a whole month off just to have a baby." Then a smile came over her tired face. "But that Tia sure is a precious baby. And so cute!"

Ding-ding! Carly turned away to greet a couple. "If a bald, red-faced, squalling brat is cute," she mumbled. "Welcome to the Dark River Diner," she said out loud. "Someone will be with you in a moment."

Aunt Frannie said, "If you'll wait on those two, I'll go make a few phone calls. Thanks, honey."

Carly put on a blue apron and picked up an order pad. "Are you ready to order?" she asked the couple, who were sitting at a booth by the window.

"Aren't you a little young to be working?" the woman asked.

"I'm just helping my aunt," Carly explained. "She and my mom own this place, and Mom's home having a baby. Well, she's already had it—now she's just resting."

The man snapped his menu shut. "What's the Dark River Special today?" he asked.

Carly turned to read it off the board. "An egg salad sandwich and tomato soup."

"Well, if Frannie says it's special, I'll try it," the man decided. The woman agreed, and Carly carried their orders back to the cook.

Ding-ding! "Welcome—oh, hi, Emma. Hi, everyone." Three girls hung up their jackets and took seats on stools at the soda fountain.

"I'll have my usual," Heather said, flipping her long blond hair. "A diet root-beer float. Just a small scoop of ice cream."

Jen's head nodded like a flower in the wind. "Me too," she said, snapping her gum.

"I'll have a regular root-beer float," Emma said. "With lots of ice cream." Carly smiled as she scooped the ice cream. Even though Heather was the most popular girl in their class, Carly liked Emma better.

Heather sniffed. "I'm not planning to wear that raincoat

forever. I want to actually look good in my swimsuit this summer. I guess some people don't care. Or else they've already given up on ever looking good." Then she and Jen giggled. Emma smiled awkwardly.

Carly's face turned red. She knew who Heather was talking about. "That'll be a dollar and sixty-five cents," she said as she plopped the float down.

Heather paid and took a long sip. "I'm going to sit by the window," she announced.

"Wait for me," Jen called as she paid for her float.

"Here's yours," Carly said to Emma. "At least you get a real float. What are you doing this afternoon? Do you want to go to the library and look through the magazines again?"

"I guess I'm just going to hang around with Heather and Jen," Emma said. "See you later."

Carly's face turned red again. But this time, she was mad. "What's the matter, dear?" Aunt Frannie asked a minute later.

"Why does everyone do whatever Heather wants? What makes her so special?"

Aunt Frannie shook her head. "It's hard to say what makes a person popular."

"Never mind," Carly said. "I know why. She's skinny and pretty. And I'm fat and ugly." With that, she stomped out the door.

"Carly," her mother called when she came in the house, "Tia wants to see you."

As she went in and sat on the couch across from her mother's rocking chair, Carly remembered the good old days. She used to come home and tell her parents all about her day. In those days, they actually cared about what happened to her and how she felt.

"Now, tell me, Carly," Mom said as she rocked back and forth gently, "how was your day?"

Carly watched her mother fuss with the baby's blanket. *Like it really matters to you now,* she thought. In a normal voice she said, "Oh, nothing much happened. They went ahead and graduated me early because I'm so smart. And I was elected Queen for the Day. Nothing special."

The baby burped. "That's nice, dear," Mom said to Carly. "And wasn't that a nice burp," she said to the baby. Carly got up and staggered to her room.

Draped across her bed, Carly talked to herself. *I wish someone could tell me what's so special about a baby. Cute? How can something that's always making a mess from one end or the other be cute?*

Then, for the first time, she said what she had been feel-

Good-For-Nothing Special

ing. "Even food gets to be special for a day at the Dark River Diner. Just for once, I'd like to be special."

But she could imagine Heather's voice. "A Dark River Special? No, Carly's more like a Good-for-Nothing Special."

TRAPPED WITH THE BABY

The rain stopped the next afternoon. Aunt Frannie threw open the diner door and took a deep breath. "Now maybe I'll get a few customers," she told Carly.

"It could still flood," Sheriff Hagerty said from his stool. "Dark River is only about two feet below the banks now. And the weather forecast is calling for thunderstorms upriver tonight. You know what that means."

Aunt Frannie frowned. "Well, maybe it won't happen. Those weather people are wrong about as often as not."

"Yeah, maybe," the sheriff said with a shake of his head. "But I wish people would be prepared, just in case. They always do the opposite of what they should in floods—they always stay in their cars and run out of their houses. Now, does that make any sense at all?"

After the sheriff left, Aunt Frannie turned to Carly. "I don't know what he's so worried about. The rain stopped."

"Is our house in danger if the river floods?"

Self-esteem; dealing with a new baby

Aunt Frannie shrugged. "Maybe, if the water gets high enough. When is your dad supposed to get back?"

"By the weekend."

Ding-ding! Emma pushed the door open. "It stopped raining. I can't believe it," she said.

"Well, get used to it," Aunt Frannie said. "It's gonna be sunny for the rest of the week. Come over here, and I'll fix both of you some hot chocolate."

A few minutes later, both girls were sitting at a booth. "Your aunt sure does make good hot chocolate," Emma said.

"Everything she makes tastes good," Carly said. "Why do you think I'm so fat?"

"You're not fat," Emma said. "You're just not thin. At least, not as thin as . . ."

"As Heather," Carly finished. "Where is she today, anyway?"

"Her mother took her shopping or something. Do you want to go to the library?"

"OK," Carly answered quickly. She loved the library, and she wanted to spend time with Emma. But inside, she was mad—mad at Emma for only being friendly when Heather wasn't around and at herself for going along with it. Then, before they got up, someone said, "So, what are you doing?" It was Heather.

Emma jumped up. "I was just hanging around," she said. "You got back early."

"Yeah, my mom changed her mind. What's going on?"

Emma laughed nervously. "I was just going to the library to look at the new magazines. Want to go?"

As they walked out, Carly put her head down on the table. Her aunt came and sat down across from her. "Carly, what's wrong?"

"Why did I have to be born fat and ugly? Everyone wants to be with Heather because she's pretty."

"Are you sure that's it?"

Carly stared at her aunt. "Come on. I'm smarter than she is—I get better grades than almost everyone in our class. I'm better than she is in sports—what else could it be?"

Aunt Frannie arranged the salt shaker and napkin holder. "Carly, people do tend to be judged by their appearance. It's more true for kids and teenagers than anyone else. But as people mature, they begin to see that beauty is more than skin deep. They begin to look for the person inside."

"I must have more than one person inside," Carly muttered, "to be this fat."

Crack! The napkin holder slammed down. "Carly, you are not fat or ugly. Stop telling yourself that. Just because you don't look like Heather doesn't mean that you won't look like Miss America when you're eighteen."

Ding-ding! Aunt Frannie got up. "Do you have any idea what your mother looked like when she was your age?" she asked. Then before Carly could say anything, Aunt Frannie turned away. "Hi, folks. Isn't that sunshine nice?"

After they were seated, Aunt Frannie came back. "Carly, I talked your mother into going shopping with me for a few minutes tonight. You'll stay home and baby-sit your little sister, won't you? It'll only be for a few minutes, until Megan can get there."

Jen's older sister, Megan, did a lot of baby-sitting. She was in high school.

"Come on. Your mother hasn't been out since Tia was born. It won't kill you to take care of her for a minute or two."

"It might," Carly grumbled. But before she knew it, her

mother was walking to Frannie's car and leaving her with the brat. "Tell Megan where the baby's formula is," she called over her shoulder. "And if—"

"Megan's been baby-sitting for years," Aunt Frannie reminded her sister. "Let's go."

Carly sat down to do her homework. *Wrriinng!* The phone rang. "Hello? Oh, hi, Megan. You'll be a little late? That's OK, she already left. No, I'll be fine. No problem."

A few minutes later, it became a problem. Tia woke up. Carly walked into the baby's room and glared over the edge of the crib. "You are a pain in the neck," she said.

Tia just gurgled and waved her arms and legs.

"What makes you so special anyway?" Carly asked quietly as she watched the baby. "You can't do anything. And you're still ugly—all babies are. Even the cute ones."

Then she reached down to straighten the blanket, and Tia grabbed her finger. "Hey, let go of that," Carly said. But she didn't pull away.

Tia squeezed and yanked softly. Then she looked up at Carly's face and almost smiled. "Hey, you like me," Carly whispered.

Wrriinng! The sound of the phone made them both jump. Carly pulled her finger away. "I'll be right back," she called as she grabbed for the phone. "Hello?"

"Carly!"

It was her mother, and Carly could tell that something was wrong. Very wrong. "Mom? What's the matter?"

"Carly, the river is flooding. Traffic is backed up at the bridge, and I can't get across."

Carly tried not to panic. "Mom, it's not even raining."

"It's been raining hard upriver. The river is flooding over

Trapped With the Baby

into town. Look outside, and see if there's water in the yard."

Carly set down the phone and raced to the front door. When she pulled it open, a wave flooded her sneakers. "Oh no!" She shoved the door shut and ran back to the phone. "Mom, the water's all the way over the steps and up to the front door."

"OK, honey, don't panic. Tell Megan that you have to—"

Click. The phone went dead.

ALMOST ALONE IN THE DARK

Mom? Mom!" Carly shook the phone and clicked the receiver. "What? What do I have to do? Mom!" But there was no sound at all from the phone.

Carly whirled around to see water pushing in under the door. "Oh no! What am I going to do?" Then she remembered. "Tia!" She raced back to Tia's bed, where the baby was quietly chewing on her blanket.

"Come on," Carly decided suddenly. "We have to go." She grabbed a blanket and wrapped the baby up tight. "We have to get out of here." Carrying the baby in her arms, Carly splashed across the now-wet carpet in the living room.

"Wait a minute," she said out loud. "We need a flashlight." She splashed over to the kitchen and opened drawers until she found a silver flashlight that worked. "Now, let's get out of here."

Before Carly could even get across the room, the electricity went out. She panicked in the total darkness until she

Self-esteem; dealing with a new baby

remembered to click on the flashlight. "It's going to be OK," she said out loud, more to herself than to Tia. Then she reached out and turned the doorknob.

Splush! A wave of water pushed the door open. Suddenly, the water in the living room was over Carly's ankles. "Oh no.

It's getting on Mom's couch! And on the books!"

Carly waded toward the bookshelf. By the time she got there, the water was halfway to her knees. Bending toward the books with the baby in her arms, Carly almost slipped and fell down. "Oh, Tia, we can't save anything. We have to get out."

But when she stood in the doorway, shining her flashlight out at the rushing water, Carly thought again. "What was it that Sheriff Hagerty said? Did he say that you should stay inside your house in a flood? Or get out?" Carly closed her eyes and prayed, "God, help me know what to do so Tia and I will be safe."

Carly opened her eyes to see the floodwaters race by and in the house. "I can't take Tia out into that. I'm staying here. I'm sure Mom will come here to look for us."

She waded back to Tia's room to find more blankets. Already, the crib was bobbing up and down with the water. Carly shifted Tia to her other arm. "We can't stay in here," she said. "Let's go back to the kitchen."

Carly settled Tia in her car seat, which was sitting on the table. Suddenly, Carly jumped. "Whoa! What was that? Something in the water bumped my leg. I hope it wasn't a snake." Somehow, Carly found herself up on the table by the baby. "We'll just wait up here for Mom," she decided.

As they waited, Carly's light began to get dimmer. "Oh no," Carly moaned. "I don't want to be here in the dark. But I might need it more later." When she clicked it off, Tia started to fuss. "Don't cry, baby." Carly slid the car seat closer and picked Tia up. "We'll be OK."

For a long time, the only sounds Carly could hear were the rushing water and the occasional bumps in the room. "I hope that's just furniture floating around," Carly said to herself. She

didn't want to think about her books, her toys, her clothes, or any creatures that might be floating by.

The water sounded closer, so Carly clicked on her light. "Tia, the water's not far below us now," she reported. "Maybe we should move to the countertop." She patted the baby on the back. "You sure are being good. I would have been screaming my head off by now. I'm so scared I still think I might."

Then Carly became aware of another noise. It was a sputtering, bubbling kind of noise. Carly had to listen for a minute before she recognized it.

"It's a boat," she decided. "And it's getting closer! Hey! Hey! We're in here!" She clicked on the flashlight and waved it at the front door and window. "Help! Help!"

Almost Alone in the Dark

The sputtering got louder, and soon a light shone through the open door. The boat noise quieted, and Sheriff Hagerty's voice bellowed, "Carly! Are you in there?"

"I'm here," Carly called. "And I have Tia."

"Hang on, we're coming to get you," the sheriff called. Soon, he waded in, wearing big rubber wading boots. "Can you hold the baby while I carry you?" he asked.

"Yes." Carly held on to Tia as Sheriff Hagerty scooped her up. "It's getting deeper," she said as he stepped out into the yard. "I'm glad I didn't try to get out by myself."

"You did exactly the right thing," he said as he set her in the boat.

The sheriff's deputy steadied the boat. "Do you want me to hold the baby?" he asked.

"No," Carly said fiercely. "She stays with me." He wrapped a coat around them both.

With everyone safely on board, the boat sputtered across the dark water. To Carly, it seemed as if the world had changed into an eerie place where trees, traffic signs, and houses floated on an endless sea. Finally, up ahead, she saw the headlights of several cars.

As the boat got closer, Carly could see people standing around those cars. Even before she got to dry land, Carly heard her mother's voice.

"Carly! Thank God they found you! Come here, baby." The hug that followed almost suffocated Carly.

"Mom! You're going to squash Tia." Carly pushed back the coat. "Are you OK?" she asked as she inspected the baby.

Mom reached out for Tia. "Oh, sweetheart! You were nice and warm in there, weren't you?" She looked up at Carly. "Where's Megan?"

"She never showed up," Carly said.

Mom nearly dropped Tia. "You were there all alone? In the flood? Oh, I'm so sorry." This hug was even tighter.

Carly tried to shrug. "I wasn't alone. Tia was with me. God was too."

As they arrived at the diner, it started to rain again. Mom ran in, carrying Tia. "Frannie, Megan never showed up. Wait until I tell you what Carly did. I'm so proud of her!"

"I'm so glad you're OK," Aunt Frannie said to Carly. "I know Megan didn't show up—she showed up here a few minutes ago. She couldn't get there because of the flood. Sheriff, Megan says that her sister Jen is at a friend's house down on Hill Street. Is that part of town flooded?"

Carly knew who lived on Hill Street—Heather did.

Almost Alone in the Dark

TRAPPED BY THE FLOOD

Sheriff Hagerty frowned. "No. It won't flood over there unless the water gets a lot higher. But someone should go get those kids now."

"I'll go get them," Megan called. "No problem."

"It will be a problem if you drive into some deep water," the sheriff growled. "Be careful."

That scared Megan a little. "Can someone go with me?"

"I can't spare anyone now," he answered. "We have to check on the houses that are already being flooded." With that, he and his deputy drove away.

Almost before she knew why, Carly said, "I'll go with you, Megan."

"Carly!" her mom nearly shouted. "You will not."

"Mom, you heard Sheriff Hagerty—there's no flooding in that part of town yet. Besides, I know what it's like to be alone out there in the dark. No one should go alone."

"Are you sure, Carly?" Aunt Frannie asked. "I know they're

Self-esteem; dealing with a new baby

your friends—sort of."

Carly nodded. Finally, Mom agreed. "If Megan promises to stay away from anything dangerous."

As she and Megan drove slowly away, all of the electricity in the town seemed to be off. Everything was dark, except where their headlights were shining. "Which way do you think we should go?" Megan asked.

"Fifth Street by the doughnut shop is the fastest," Carly said.

As they turned onto Fifth Street, Carly gasped. "Look!" There, just beyond the edge of the street, the light reflected off floodwater. Megan pushed the gas pedal.

Before long, they were banging on the door of Heather's house. "Hey, anyone home?" Megan called. "Jen, are you there?"

On the second floor a window slid open, and a face popped out. "Who is it?" Heather called.

"It's Megan. Tell Jen she has to go now. The town is flooding!"

"Really? Great!" Heather pulled her head back inside. "Come on, Jen," she called. "Your sister's here. She says there's a flood."

Before long, they rushed out the front door—Heather, Jen, and Emma. "Where are your parents?" Megan asked Heather.

"Oh, they went into town to shop," Heather responded. "They won't be back for hours."

"You can say that again," Megan said. "They may not be able to get back at all tonight. I think you'd all better come with me to the diner. Then we can ask Sheriff Hagerty to contact your parents."

Heather climbed into the front seat, so Carly got in back with Jen and Emma. "Is it really bad out there?" Emma asked Carly. She seemed frightened.

"I hope so," Heather interrupted. "Do you think the school is flooded?" She turned to Megan. "Let's go by the school and see if it's underwater."

"I don't know if that would be safe," Megan said.

"Sure it would be," Heather urged. "If we see any deep water, we'll just turn around. You guys want to go, don't you?"

"Yeah," Jen said. "Let's do it." Emma didn't say anything. Carly shook her head.

"Well, I guess it would be OK," Megan said slowly as she turned that direction. "We'll be careful." Everything seemed normal as they sped along, except for the darkness. Only a few flashlights and lanterns showed along the streets.

"I don't see any flood. I don't even see any water," Heather complained as they turned onto the street leading to the school. "Are you guys sure . . . Whoa!"

Suddenly, the street in front of them turned into a river. Water was rushing across as though it was in a hurry to get somewhere. "That's amazing," Heather said. "But look, it's not up to the school yet."

They could see the school on the other side of the water. Water was just lapping the bottom of the steps leading up to the front door. "Let's drive over there," Heather said.

"Are you crazy?" Carly shouted. "Let's get out of here." Megan looked from one to the other.

"It can't be deep," Heather argued. "You can see where it stops on the other side. Come on, just go. You want to, don't you, Jen?"

"Sure," Jen said, snapping her gum. "Let's go for it." Megan shrugged and started forward slowly. The water touched the tires, then climbed as they went forward. Carly could feel her fingernails digging into her palms, but she couldn't relax. "God," she prayed silently, "I can't stop them. Please keep us safe."

"Look, we're more than halfway across," Heather said, looking out her window. "With water all around us, it looks like we're floating." A sudden movement bumped her head against the glass. "Now it feels like we're floating."

"That's because we are," Megan said in a frightened voice. She slammed on the brakes, and the car stopped, bounced, and started floating sideways again. "I can't make it stop," Megan screamed.

While Heather and Jen joined in the screaming, Carly tried to think. *What did Sheriff Hagerty say about being in a car in a flood?* Then she remembered. When she opened her door, the screaming stopped for a second. "We have to get out," she shouted.

Trapped by the Flood

"Are you sure?" Emma asked.

"We have to," Carly repeated. "Come on! If we stick to-gether, we can still make it to the school." She pulled Emma out, then reached for Heather. Heather seemed frozen with fear. "Come on, Heather. The car's going to float off into the ditch any second."

Finally, Megan shoved and Carly pulled until Heather was out. Megan and Jen scrambled out just as the car tipped and fell over into deeper water.

When Heather started to scream again, Carly grabbed her by the arm. "Stop it!" she shouted. "We don't have time for that. Come on, everyone, hold on to each other." With only

Carly's dim flashlight and the headlights sticking up to guide them, they waded forward toward the school.

When the water was higher than their knees, Emma slipped. "Help!" she screamed. With Megan's help, Carly grabbed her and helped her back up. Then the water began to get shallower until they reached the steps. The bottom step was covered, but the girls climbed the other five and collapsed at the top.

As they watched, Megan's car rolled the rest of the way over, and its headlights disappeared. Megan put her head down and sobbed. "What do we do now?" Emma whispered.

"We wait," Carly answered. She pointed her flashlight down at the water for a second, then clicked it off. It was nearly dead, anyway. "And we hope someone finds us soon. The water is already over the second step."

SOMEONE SPECIAL

I t's so dark," Emma whispered. She had crawled over to sit beside Carly on the top step. "I never imagined what our town would look like without any lights. It's so scary."

"At least we're not alone," Carly said. "When I was trapped at home, the only person with me was Tia. And she didn't say much to make me feel better."

Behind them, the only sounds were Megan's sobbing and Jen's gum snapping. In front of them, the water swished and rumbled. Suddenly, Emma jerked her feet up. "What was that? Something touched my foot!"

Carly jumped up and snapped on her light. With its dim glow, she couldn't see much. But she could see that the water was rising fast. "It must have been the water. It's up to the fifth step."

"What are we going to do when it gets this high?" Emma asked in a shaky voice.

Self-esteem; dealing with a new baby

"We're going to drown," Heather wailed from where she sat. "I just know we are."

"Not me," Carly replied. "There's got to be a way into the school. Or better yet, onto the top of it. Emma, if you stand on my shoulders, can you reach the edge of the roof?"

Jen's gum popped louder. "Hey, look," she said. "A light."

They all turned and stared as a single light floated on the water a distance away. "What is it?" Emma asked.

Then Carly heard it. It was a sputtering, bubbling kind of sound. "It's Sheriff Hagerty's boat!" She began to wave her light and shout. "Hey! Over here!"

The light turned toward them. "Hold on, ladies," the sheriff's voice said over a megaphone. "We're coming."

When the boat got close enough, the light focused on

Carly. "Say, haven't I already rescued you once tonight?" the sheriff asked.

"Yes, sir," Carly answered with a laugh. "Remember, Megan was going to pick up her sister, and you told her to watch out for deep water? I volunteered to go with her."

"Well, I can see you found deep water. Looks like you

found the sister, too, along with a couple of spares. What happened?"

"We tried to drive through some water, and the car started floating. We jumped out and waded over here."

He shook his head. "It's a good thing you got out. That car may be halfway down the river by now. All right, let's get aboard. I've got other people to rescue tonight."

By now, the Dark River diner was lit up with half-a-dozen lanterns. It was full of worried people, including Emma's mom and Heather's parents. Carly's mother wrapped her up in a big hug. "I'm not letting you go again."

"Don't worry, Mom. I'm staying here. The water won't get this high, will it?"

"No. Sheriff Hagerty says it's starting to go down now. The worst is past. We'll be a little crowded, because a lot of people are staying here until they can get back to their homes. Come on. I'll find you something to eat, and we can check on Tia."

While her mother was making sandwiches in the kitchen, Carly stared at pictures in her aunt's living room, where Tia was asleep. The flickering light made them seem different from the way she remembered them.

"Mom," she asked as she walked into the kitchen, "is it really you in that picture? Beside Aunt Frannie at the fair?"

Mom looked up and grinned. "Yes, when I was about your age. But I was having a bad hair day. Why do you ask?"

"You just look so plain," Carly said softly. "Not pretty, like you do now."

"Carly, I'm not a beautiful woman. I'm normal. I look fine when I'm happy and I've had enough sleep. But that's the way most people are. In those days, I looked a lot like you do now."

"Does that mean I'll look like you when I grow up?" Carly asked shyly.

"Probably," Mom agreed. "But not exactly. You may not win beauty contests or be a model, but you'll always be a smart, caring person. And your friends will always love you for being the special person that you are."

"Thanks, Mom."

Ding-ding! A few days later, the bell on the diner door was ringing steadily. It seemed that everyone had a flood story to share, and it sounded best over a slice of apple pie or a Dark River Special.

With school still closed, Carly was wearing a blue apron and working at the soda fountain. Her mom and dad were home scraping mud out of the house. "Here are your sundaes, sir."

As she made change for the five dollar bill the man gave her, Carly saw Heather, Jen, and Emma slip through the open door. They headed straight for the stools in front of her.

"What a day!" Heather said, flipping her hair. "I'll have my usual. No, make it regular root-beer float. Any day that the school is closed is a day to celebrate."

"Me too," Jen said. Emma nodded her head also.

With a sigh, Carly turned to scoop the ice cream. When she handed over the floats, Heather flashed a big smile. "I'm glad I don't have to work today."

Carly clenched her teeth. "That will be a dollar sixty-five cents each."

Heather turned to her friends. "I'm going to watch them cut up those trees that fell over in the park. Let's go."

"Wait for me," Jen called, pulling change out of her pocket.

"I'm going to hang out here with Carly," Emma said. All

three girls turned and stared. "I think it would be fun to work in a diner."

Heather flipped her hair. "Me and my friends are leaving," she said.

Emma shrugged. "Carly, do you think your aunt would let me hang around? I could help with whatever you have to do." She didn't even look up when the diner door dinged shut. "And maybe I could wear one of those aprons."

Carly could only smile. "Let's ask her."

"Hey," someone by the window called, "the sun is out! Look!"

A ray of sunshine burst through the clouds, through the diner window, and right across where Carly was standing. Just for a moment, her smile was the brightest, most beautiful thing in town.

The Hard Way

We're going to make a ton of money," Daniel bragged as he pedaled. "That old dump is full of aluminum cans, and when we turn them in for recycling, we'll have enough money to last all summer."

"I hope you're right," Jose said as they coasted into Mike's yard on their bikes. "Hey, Mike, you ready to go?"

Mike popped out the door and walked over to them with one hand behind his back. "You guys want to see something?" he asked.

"Sure," Daniel said. "Is it something we're taking to the dump with us?"

"I'd like to," Mike answered. Then he pulled it out.

"Hey, that's a gun," Jose said. "What are you doing with it?"

"A gun!" Daniel echoed. "Cool! Can I see it?"

Mike held it out, one finger on the trigger guard. "It's my dad's pistol," he explained. "He uses it to target shoot—and to

Dealing with guns

kill water moccasins when he goes fishing. Do you like it?" He pointed it toward them as he asked.

"Stop that!" Jose shouted. "Don't you know anything about guns? Stop pointing that thing at us!"

"Oh, stop whining," Mike said. "It's not loaded."

"We're leaving," Jose said quickly. "Come on, Daniel."

Daniel still wanted to look at the gun. "But, Jose, I just wanted to—"

Jose cut him off. "I'm leaving now. Mike, we'll meet you at the dump—without that gun." Then he spun his bike around and took off. After a second of hesitation, Daniel followed him.

"Why didn't you want to look at it, Jose?" he asked as he rode along beside.

"That wasn't a toy," Jose said. "That pistol could kill you."

"But Mike said it wasn't loaded."

Jose shook his head. "My dad says that lots of people get killed every day by guns that aren't loaded. At least, someone thinks they aren't loaded. But when the trigger is pulled, they find out they were wrong—dead wrong."

The dump lived up to its name. Bottles, cans, pieces of old furniture, and stuff were scattered everywhere. "There's an aluminum can," Jose said. "And there's another. You were right about this place."

Before they had many cans, Mike rode up. "So, did you find much?" He was carrying a rifle.

"Hey, I told you—"

Mike held up his hand. "Relax, Jose. This is just my BB gun. I only brought it along for protection. From rats or bees or whatever."

"Wow, a BB gun," Daniel said. He ran over to see it up close. "Can I try a shot or two?"

"Maybe later. If we can find something to shoot at," Mike answered. For a while, the boys kept busy, picking up the scattered aluminum cans and stuffing them in their bags. Then Daniel saw something move. Something big!

"Whoa! What was that?" he shouted, jumping up on an old washing machine. Then he saw it again. "It's a rat!"

"Keep an eye on it," Mike said. He ran over to his bike, grabbed the BB gun, and raced back, cocking the gun as he ran.

"Hey, watch it!" Jose yelled as the gun went right past his face.

"There he goes," Daniel reported. The rat ran. Mike pulled the trigger. *Snap!* The BB bounced off a tin can. Mike cocked

the gun and shot again. *Crack!* The BB broke an old peanut butter jar.

"You missed him," Jose said as the rat disappeared inside a molding couch.

"But look at that jar," Mike said. "It cracked in half. Good shot, huh?"

"Let me try it," Daniel asked.

"Wait. Let's set up several bottles on this box and shoot at them," Mike answered. He began to line up dirty old bottles on the box. Daniel started to help him.

"I'm not so sure that's a good idea," Jose said. "This is not our property. It might not be safe to shoot at glass like that."

"What's wrong with breaking a few bottles?" Mike asked. "Besides, this dump doesn't belong to anyone."

"Well, the BB could bounce back and hit someone. Or a glass could shatter and cut someone," Jose said.

Mike laughed at Jose. "What are you, some kind of chicken? I've done this lots of times." He aimed at the first bottle and fired. *Crack!* The bottle's pieces slid to the ground. "Now, watch me break that big green one."

Pooff! Nothing happened. "I must be out of BBs." Mike shook the gun. There was no rattling sound. "Too bad."

"Aw, I wanted to shoot," Daniel complained. With a sigh, he went back to looking for cans. He found a bunch of them next to a big crate. "Hey, guys, here's a ton of them. Bring another bag." Then he heard a sound that made him spin around.

Buzzzz! "Whoa!" he shouted as he dodged away.

"What is it?" Mike shouted. "Another rat?"

Daniel stopped when he got to where Jose was. "No, it's a wasp—I mean a bunch of them. On a big nest."

"Where?" Mike wanted to see it.

"Right inside that crate," Daniel reported. "See, right in the corner."

Mike picked up his gun and stepped closer. "Boy, if I had more BBs, I'd show those wasps a thing or two." He peered inside the crate. "I could just stand here  and pick them off one at a time." He cocked the gun and aimed. "Yeah, I got 'em right in my sights."

He pulled the trigger. *Snap!* A BB shot out. *Crack!* It hit the wasp nest. Wasps went everywhere!

"Yikes!" Mike shouted. "Run!"

Daniel and Jose were already running. But not far. Daniel's foot hit a piece of wire. He hit the ground. "Ooof! Ow!"

Jose tripped over an old bucket. "Whoa!" he shouted as he fell. *Crack!* His hand hit a glass jar.

When they finally made it back to their bikes, Mike had been stung twice, Daniel had a scrape on his arm, and Jose was dripping blood from a cut on his hand. "Come on," Jose said, pressing his hand against his shirt, "my mom's home." They rode slowly and shakily to Jose's house.

Jose's mother teased them. "I don't know who started this war, but I can see who lost. What did the other guys look like?"

"They were this big," Daniel reported, holding his fingers about an inch apart, "red, and they had wings. And they were mad." He thumped Mike's arm. "Thanks to you!"

"Hey, I didn't think I could really hit their nest. I didn't even think the BB gun was loaded!"

After everyone had been cleaned up and treated, they retired to the front porch to eat Popsicles. "Maybe my dad will help us get our bags of cans when he gets home," Jose said.

Mike stood up. "Well, would you guys get my gun too? I don't really want to go back there today." Jose nodded, and Mike rode away. Slowly.

Daniel shook his head. "I guess you were right about guns that aren't loaded. Look what happened to us—and it was just a BB gun that wasn't loaded!" He sighed. "But I never got to try shooting."

"You can shoot mine sometime," Jose said.

"You have a BB gun?"

Jose nodded. "But I can only shoot it when my dad's around. Let's see if he'll set up some targets for us in the backyard after we get the cans from the dump."

Daniel's face broke into a grin. Then it clouded over. "Do

you think he'll do that after he finds out about today? And what happened at the dump?"

Jose laughed. "He'll think we learned a good lesson. The hard way."

Daniel nodded. "I guess we did."

Being Smart Around Guns

1. If someone is playing with a gun, leave immediately. And tell a grown-up.
2. Treat every gun as if it were loaded—always point it in a safe direction, and keep it open or uncocked, except when you are going to shoot.
3. If you're going to shoot a gun, take gun-shooting and safety lessons first.
4. Never shoot a gun unless a grown-up is present.
5. Shoot at safe targets. Make sure that what's behind the target can't be hurt, either.